Daikaiju Yuki

ISBN: 978-0692876671

First Edition: May 2017

Special Thanks

My beta readers, including Klen Hautzenroder, Alex Gayhart, Janet Sheffer, and Lawrence and Julia Coronelli.

Additional thanks to Steven Sloss and the Kaijusaurus Podcast, Halley Eveland, William Cope, Garett Gillette, Michael Callari, Jason Vickers, the rest of the kaiju krew, G-Fest and its organizers, and very large monsters everywhere.

In memory of Yuki, my cat.

By Raffael Coronelli

Chapter 1:

Yuki Lives

Well, she thought, *here we go.*

The eyes of the gleaming gold lion statue seemed to stare down at her with solemn severity from its perch atop the massive red archway. Beyond the gate loomed the shape of a gigantic pagoda, covered in solid gold finish. Towering a hundred meters into the air, it was said to mirror the exact height of Narai's guardian monster.

It was the Temple of Narajin – the lion kaiju, guardian of Narai, and one of the five Pantheon Colossi. A masterpiece of construction, his temple had stood for the five millennia the god had slumbered, and was the symbol of Narai City, Yuki's home.

An aroma of cherry blossoms overwhelmed her senses. The beauty before her – white flowers hanging on the trees that lined the path from the gate to the glorious pagoda – was in stark contrast to any of the gut-wrenching images she had seen in the last few days. How, she thought, could life and beauty continue like this when such horrible things occurred? It made her want to be sick.

She had no idea what exactly she was about to find, but at least this mission was away from the battlefield and the images it had burned onto her inner eye forever. Mountainous beings advancing ahead of an oncoming army, the gods of the Earth and legends of old returned to wage a new war.

Standing below the entrance, she checked her uniform to make sure she looked presentable. Her shirt was drenched in sweat from the journey, the muggy, humid air attacking her pores with the voracity of a full-scale invasion. It didn't take long to realize that she smelled horrible, but there wasn't much she could do about that now.

"Son of a bitch," she muttered to herself.

Still stiff, she lifted her arms out to the sides and rolled her shoulders. It felt good to stretch her muscles after being stuck in the cramped military transport for so long, bringing her fists in toward her chest and letting her powerful biceps flex through the tight tunic sleeves. Reaching back, she adjusted her small hair bun, making sure it was firmly in place. When worn down, it was roughly neck-length, making it just long enough to tie up in standard military fashion. Looking up, she saw that the sky shone blue and bright, with only a few wispy clouds passing between the life-giving rays of the sun and the Earth below. It reminded her of how lucky she was to still have her life, something that so many of her compatriots could not say for themselves. In spite of everything that had happened, she was alive.

Giving one more glance toward the statue of the lion, she stepped under the arch and started down the path toward the temple. The paved trail was bordered by trees hung with sakura blossoms, periodically falling to the ground and scattering themselves before her. Traveling through it was like moving along a floral tunnel that made her feel like she was slowly progressing further and further into some kind of artfully arranged dream.

Now that she was moving, her legs quickly lost stiffness. So they should, she thought. A decade of combat training had sculpted her into a hundred and fifty centimeters of deadly force. The strength she most needed now, however, was strength of mind.

Looking down the end of the path as she neared the entrance to the pagoda, she could see the silhouette of a person standing on the front steps looking out at her. This immediately made her feel uncomfortable, knowing that she was in some way expected. Drawing closer, she saw that it was the figure of a tall woman in a white and grey kimono.

The specter seemed to hold herself with impeccably controlled posture, and had a slender figure and long, black hair that draped straight down past her shoulders and onto her back. She seemed to be in her early to mid thirties, slightly older than Yuki but not by much. The curvature of her features, dark eyelashes, and immaculate complexion lead Yuki to believe in that moment – although she wasn't sure if it was just her mind being overwhelmed by delirium – that she was the most beautiful woman she had ever seen.

This, more than anything, frightened Yuki. She knew that in her current state, she looked disheveled at best and a sweat stained wreck at worst. The fact that she was being confronted by an unbelievably attractive member of the same sex was absolutely nerve-wracking.

Yuki slowly neared the foot of the long row of wooden steps, the woman standing on the fifth level just above her, still motionless, still staring intently. Yuki quickly descended into a deep bow, mostly out of a desire to avoid eye contact.

"As Priestess of Narajin," said the woman in a low and commanding tone, "I welcome you to his temple."

Rising to look at her, Yuki decided that getting straight to the point was the most pertinent order of business.

"Tsubaki Yuki, Lieutenant, Narai army," she introduced herself, surname first, in as serious and direct a manner as she could muster. "I'm here to inquire about the whereabouts of Major Sakurai... I... understand that he's with you?"

The Priestess' gaze pierced through her, a warm expression on her face but still not letting on exactly where she stood on the issue.

"Major Sakurai is no longer with us," she said.

"No longer with you?" Yuki asked, baffled. "Do... you know where he went?"

"I'm sorry," said the Priestess, her brow furrowing. "I'm not sure what help to you I can be. Sakurai stayed with us for a few days, then left to continue his mission elsewhere."

"But..." Yuki had never been more confused. "My direct orders were to find him here, and report back with his progress. I can't leave empty-handed."

"Do you know what his mission was?" the Priestess asked coldly.

"I... actually have no idea. I was hoping to find out for myself."

Yuki truthfully didn't have the slightest idea what was going on, and was not keeping anything from the woman who seemed to be interrogating her as much as vice versa. The Priestess, on the other hand, was clearly not coming forward with everything that she knew, a fact that frustrated her tremendously.

Perhaps sensing that Yuki was being genuine, the Priestess' demeanor grew warmer, a gentle smile breaking across her face.

"Why don't you stay with us for a while," she said. "We could use a new member of the temple staff for a few days. Maybe you'll find what you're looking for in that time, or maybe you'll find some other type of fulfillment."

Unsure of how to respond to the offer, Yuki remained silent.

"Here," continued the Priestess, reaching into a pocket in her robe. "I've got something for you."

Slowly and gracefully, she descended the steps toward Yuki. Stopping in front of her, she held out her hand, nodding for Yuki to do the same. A black teardrop-shaped stone, about six centimeters long and with a surface so polished it reflected the sunlight, dropped into Yuki's palm.

"Everyone in the temple has one of these," she said, still smiling and looking at Yuki with an expression that she was having trouble deciphering.

"What is it?" Yuki asked hesitantly.

"It's a token of your connection to Narajin himself. There's more to it than that, but I'd suggest that you hold onto it. You're actually lucky – these only used to end up in the hands of the higher ups here, but these days it's hard to find anyone who really wants to dedicate their lives to a guardian monster."

"Did Ken Sakurai have one of these?" Yuki asked, dropping all honorifics to be as direct as possible.

Staring intently, the Priestess seemed to be trying to read Yuki further, as if second guessing her decision to give her the trinket.

"Ken chose his own path," she said at last. "I think you would choose another."

"What..." said Yuki, starting to feel slightly threatened.

The Priestess burst into laughter, covering her mouth with her hand and flashing Yuki a sly look with her eyes. The woman had done nothing but make Yuki feel confused and uncomfortable since she had arrived, mostly from the combination of her sharp good looks, confident behavior, and the indecipherable messages she seemed to be sending.

Get it together, Yuki, she thought to herself.

"Alright," said the Priestess, stepping to the side, "I'll let you get situated. Meet me here tomorrow morning and we can continue your acclimation."

Bowing once more, Yuki climbed the stairs to the massive pagoda's doorway, standing for a moment just outside. With a deep breath, she entered.

The first order of business was picking up her temple uniform. The second was bathing – she needed to wash herself after the long, sweaty day of travel, and could tell that her smell wasn't making her popular by the looks of everyone she passed making her way down the wood-lined hallway to the other side of the temple.

There were private bathing areas reserved for higher-ups like the Priestess, but the communal bath was outdoors toward the back of the temple grounds, or so she was told by the person who had given her the uniform. Sure enough, walking out the back steps of the pagoda, she saw a small, winding path leading through the back garden. At the end of it, at the foot of a hill on the edge of the Temple grounds was a large, shimmering pool, into which flowed a waterfall from some overhanging rocks. Fortunately, she had entire thing to herself, but she still had the sneaking feeling that eyes were watching her – the newcomer, the second arrived purveyor of violence from the losing side of a war, encroaching on a place of peace.

Blocking this idea out of her mind, she slipped behind the changing screen that stood between the pool and the view of the pagoda. She reached back and undid her bun, letting her hair loose just as a refreshing breeze blew through it. With a surprising amount of effort, she peeled away her shirt and lifted it off of her body. It was the first time since the previous day that she had gotten a chance to get out of her clothes, and she could not be happier to be rid of them – stench and all. Stepping out of her uniform pants, she dipped in her left foot before descending into the warm pool.

Water flowed around her, refreshing and rejuvenating her physically and mentally. She tried to blank out her mind and exist only in the moment – the soothing sensation of having her body submerged in the hot spring, the rising steam flowing past her face. It was the exact opposite of the awful things she had seen, and was exactly what she needed.

Closing her eyes, she was greeted by the memory of the tip of a great toothed beak descending from above and clamping around the upper torso of Commander Ito, her superior officer, slicing him in two midway down his spinal column. Eyes flying open, she winced in disgust. Forgetting that would not be easy.

The Commander of the forward Narai legion had been killed by Alkonoth, the hundred-meter-tall ibis goddess of the Scythian Empire to the north. Her slender form and purposeful movements had been terrifying to behold during her attack on Narai's northernmost island alongside the bear kaiju Mokwa, sent by Scythia's ally Laurentia on the far side of the world.

Inhaling deeply and deliberately, she drew the steamy air into her lungs, then let it out as if expelling the bad memories from her mind. Her hands ran slowly over her skin, wiping the remnants of grime from her pores and freeing her from their grasp. It almost felt as if the ritual was giving her strength, increasing her vitality.

Wading to the other side of the pool and slipping under the waterfall, she let the cold mountain water flow over her, washing any remaining debris from her hair and face. The longer she stayed under, the more the horror slipped away into the pool of distant memory.

Just keep going, she thought to herself. *You just have to keep going.*

Stepping out of the pool, she grabbed her towel and dried herself off before slipping into the plain white and cream colored robe she had been given. They were unsurprisingly more comfortable than what she had been wearing before, and the strange sensation of having clean clothing draped around her felt almost like a novelty.

The uniform out of which she had changed seemed to stare back at her from the mat where she had left it. With silent indignation, she picked it up, carried it out with her as she stepped into her outdoor sandals, and deposited them in a nearby waste receptacle. There wasn't a place to keep her personal affects in the Temple, aside from on her person. If she was to be scolded for anything upon her return to the military, assuming there would be a military to return to, losing a fellow officer and failing her mission would be far more grave than getting rid of her uniform.

Feeling momentarily relieved, she tucked the small stone the Priestess had given her into the pocket of her new garments and started down the path toward the back entrance to the pagoda that glistened as the sun set into the west to her left.

By the time she had stepped into her indoor slippers and made her way to the mess hall, she realized that it was far later than she had anticipated. Everyone had left, leaving her to eat the leftover onigiri in the kitchen. It was fine, of course. She didn't feel like talking to anyone, and even at the worst, what she was left with was far better than military rations.

When she was done, she began the seemingly endless climb up the winding staircase to her quarters on the fourteenth floor. It was a communal sleeping area with a large tatami mat that at least ten other temple workers lay on, already asleep – or at least pretending to be to avoid interacting with her. Bathed in the moonlight that streamed in through the open window, the sound of cicadas floating in from outside, she went to the wardrobe where she found her night robes, stepped behind the changing screen and emerged moments later.

Delicately as she could, she stepped over the others and made her way to an open spot on the mat that had been prepared with a pillow and blanket, and lay down. Despite her supremely exhausted state, falling asleep proved difficult.

That day had felt like it had lasted a year, and enough had transpired to warrant the feeling. For the first time in her life, she had absolutely no idea what she was going to do. At least she had met an interesting woman who seemed to show some type of interest in her, whatever that may be. She wasn't entirely sure how people here would treat her, but if the Priestess was any indication, she expected lots of indecipherable mixed messages. The mystery of what happened to Ken was even more mind-boggling.

Ken had been part of her circle of friends during their first years in the army, before he ascended past her level, and was the only member of their training platoon who hadn't been killed. Some said he had gotten in deep with the Narai military's inner circle and was privy to things that would horrify most people, but she wasn't sure she believed it. Deep down, she hoped it wasn't true. Perhaps that was why she volunteered for the mission herself, to find out where the intentions of her old friend lay.

Great, she thought.

Dealing with people wasn't something she was entirely good at, despite her popularity among the other girls in the army. She could understand them, though. They liked her, she liked them, and none of them asked a lot of questions. Any kind of lasting relationship was more or less impossible in that environment, which suited Yuki just fine. It was purely physical, and it was fun. Here, she assumed, she wouldn't be doing a lot of that. Too bad, since the Priestess really had struck her as attractive. As recent memories went, that wasn't a bad one to focus on.

Her hand drifted into her pocket and found the stone that the woman had given her. However insignificant a trinket it seemed, the woman had shown kindness to her, and that was something to cherish on its own.

As her hand brushed against the small object, a strange feeling washed over her, one she couldn't quite place. It was an unfamiliar presence – a memory of a forgotten dream that she didn't remember having – a locked door in her mind that she never realized was there.

Before she could give it any more thought, she drifted into sleep.

Chapter 2:
Ritual

As Yuki gently emerged from the dreamless night, she was greeted by the sound of running water, singing birds, and a soft breeze coming in through the window. The first, faint rays of dawn hitting the wooden floor next to her told her that it was still early – something her regimen had instilled into her. No one else in the communal sleeping quarters had yet awakened, giving her a momentary sense of accomplishment.

Climbing to her feet, she quickly changed into her temple robes, stepped into her hall slippers and started across the creaky wooden hallway of the fourteenth floor toward the stairwell. With any luck, she would reach the front garden before the Priestess.

The inside of the temple was completely empty, filled only by Yuki and the gentle, etherial first light of the day streaming through the small windows in the sides of the stairwell. Each step echoed a creak in the floorboards, deafening next to the otherwise dead silence. It would've been unnerving if not for how much she had on her mind.

Rounding the last bend in the stairwell, warm light flooded in through the open front door of the pagoda. It took her eyes a moment to adjust before the colors of the outside vista struck them with vivid intensity. The garden stretched from the front of the pagoda all the way to the gate, blooming with precisely organized sections of different colored flowers. Perfectly geometric stripes of red, white, yellow, pink, and blue lay spread out like an enormous painting.

Stepping out, she was completely overwhelmed by the beauty of seeing it full-on without the distraction of being deliriously tired as she had been the last afternoon. What surprised her the most, however, was that it was not empty, and she was not the first one outside.

Crouching down on the side of the main path, tending to a row of blue flowers, was a woman she instantly recognized as the Priestess. Unlike the plain white and grey kimono she had worn the day before, a blue and gold one that matched the color of the flowers beside which she knelt draped around her. The Priestess looked up from the garden and flashed a smile at her.

"Hello Yuki," she she said in her typically gentle, yet perfectly controlled tone.

Completely taken aback and tongue tied by her presence, Yuki tried to figure out how to respond. Her plan of getting information from her was slipping away, and she had no idea what type of strategy to form for the current circumstances, especially with how glamorous the Priestess managed to look while digging around in the dirt.

"Come," the Priestess beckoned with her free hand, "the flowers look better up close."

Apprehensive, Yuki climbed down the steps and onto the main path, approaching the woman through the garden but trying to maintain a safe distance.

"Good morning, Priestess," Yuki began.

"You look like you've rested well," the Priestess responded, smile still hanging across her face. "Not that you didn't look good before... What I mean is..."

She put her hand in front of her face and laughed softly, as if embarrassed by her own remarks. As before, Yuki was completely flabbergasted.

"Thank you," Yuki replied smoothly. "You look beautiful."

The words slipped out before Yuki had any idea what she was saying, but she played off the strong complement as casually as she could.

"Well, that's very nice of you," said the Priestess, her smile turning to a sly grin.

As much as Yuki wanted to keep being suspicious, the Priestess gave off such a warm, understanding aura that it was hard to stay tense. Still, she somehow found a way, as her heart pounded into her throat while she tried to formulate a convincing way to ask the questions she was looking for.

"I'm still confused about..."

"Major Sakurai?" said the Priestess in a slightly disappointed tone. "Just trying to soften me up, then."

"No!" Yuki blurted out. "I just... have to know."

The Priestess laughed again, then sighed and stood up slowly, looking up at the sky as if trying to think of what to say.

"As before," she said at last, "he's no longer here."

"And you don't know where he is?" said Yuki facetiously. "I hope you know I don't buy that."

The woman looked down, as if trying not to show that the questions were making her uncomfortable.

"I'm sorry," Yuki continued, making an effort to sound less abrasive. "I don't know what his mission was... whatever it was, it's not mine."

Pausing, she took a deep breath.

"What did he try to do?"

"Nothing that matters now," the Priestess said softly, seeming to force another smile. "No harm was done. Look."

The woman extended her left arm toward Yuki, motioning to the garden with the other.

"I want to show you something."

Feeling slightly more at ease with her companion, even if the issue was still unresolved, Yuki stepped closer.

"We try to make the garden completely symmetrical," the Priestess began. "Each type of flower gets exactly the same amount of space as the others. Every day I come out here and tend to them, making sure their arrangement is perfect. It's become a sort of ritual."

She reached down and picked a yellow flower Yuki hadn't even noticed that had been growing amidst the blue. The Priestess handed it to her with a smile.

"For all their beauty and symmetry," she continued, "they're wild, living things. They'll grow wherever they please, and try as you might, you can't force them to do otherwise."

Yuki couldn't believe that the woman before her was making her identify with a plant, but that was exactly what was happening.

"Perfection is always an illusion, and the more you try to reach it, the more you risk breaking yourself. Like a flower, the beauty of a living being lies in the vibrance with which it lives. Other yellow flowers will grow where we've planted the blue ones. They won't stay within the lines because they don't need to. They don't worry about pleasing those who want to confine them. They simply are."

Feeling half enlightened and half bewildered, Yuki joined the Priestess in her gardening ritual, tending to dead flowers and trying her best to arrange them in the face of everything she had just been told to the contrary. The two of them didn't talk about much of anything for the rest of the morning, but it was still nice to have the company of someone she liked.

Her entire life, she had been preparing for the strict regimen of the military. Precise strategies and perfect execution were her speciality, and no one disciplined her harder for failing to live up to an impossible standard than she did. Her whole life, she had been trying to live up to the legacy of her father and be the new Toshiro Tsubaki, the greatest soldier in Narai. She had barely considered that she might have a completely different path ahead of her.

That much was now obvious at this point – the awful experience of being a soldier on the ground when kaiju were attacking was just too much for anyone to handle and come out intact. Still, she never thought she'd rather be gardening instead.

That thought struck her with the impact of a kaiju's footfall – she was gardening, comparing her life to a flower. The Priestess' speech was everything she hated hearing – *everyone is special, everyone has to choose their own path, do what makes you happy*... It made her want to vomit. The worst part was that as wimpy as she felt admitting it to herself, the Priestess was right. There was something no one had planned for her that she had to do if she was going to do something more impactful with her life than garden. Not that gardening was actually that bad... It was kind of peaceful and helped put her mind at ease.

Damn...

After meeting in the main hall for lunch with the rest of the temple's staff, she was assigned to the library for the afternoon. Located on the top floor of the pagoda, the temple library was where copies of Narai's most important manuscripts were kept, some supposedly dating back to the time the five nations were founded. It was a vast room with light only let in through screens, so as not to fade the inscriptions on the books and scrolls. Yuki had been assigned to organize a section devoted to biographical records of government leaders, but there was hardly anyone else around and she doubted anyone would really notice if she skipped it.

She wandered slowly through the rows of shelves, looking over the dusty volumes that contained the long and storied history of her people. The smell of books was welcome and familiar, as military life involved so much waiting and dead time that she regularly read just to keep herself sane – mostly historical fiction set in the Anno period, a fascination of hers.

One after another, she read the titles of the volumes as she passed. One, that she briefly flipped through before putting back out of fear for the pages crumbling from the spine, contained transcriptions of first-hand accounts from the first kaiju war from which Narajin and the rest of the Pantheon Colossi had emerged. Another documented an explorer's journey to some far-off land called Alkebulan, a contemporary human civilization that existed outside the five nations – one of many, to be sure.

Suddenly, the spine of one book in particular caught her eye on a high shelf. There were no words, just a vague, almost worn-off picture of an elongated oval, sparking her to wonder if the shape being depicted was in any way analogous to the trinket she had been given by the Priestess. Pulling the small object out of her kimono, she turned it slowly between her fingers, inspecting it as her mind drifted to an unfamiliar, barely defined place once more. Looking up at the book, she wanted answers but realized that it was far outside the extent of her arms.

"That's an interesting one," an elderly man's voice announced from the end of the row of shelves.

Yuki practically jumped through the ceiling in surprise, turning to see the library master Eiichi. He was a short old man who might have been much taller before his spine had contracted into an arch. He wore the same soft smile as he had in their every interaction, at peace with the world and the insurmountable amount of knowledge he possessed on it.

"I'm sorry sir," Yuki began, still flustered, "I didn't mean to –"

"Oh don't worry, those biographies practically sort themselves. If someone really wants to read about Emperor Kaneko, they'll have no problem finding him. Of much more worth are these..." he motioned to the book he cradled in his arms, "astronomical discoveries of the old world. Their impossible machines may have long since crumbled, but knowledge lives forever!"

"Mr. Eiichi," she asked suddenly.

"You can drop the honorific," he said, "we're all the same here. This isn't the army, you know."

"Alright... Why was a soldier on a mission here?"

The old man paused for a moment, raising his eyebrows.

"You mean to ask what it is you're doing here yourself?"

"No," she said. "What was Major Sakurai doing here?"

"Asking questions is a sign of perception."

"What's that supposed to mean?" asked Yuki, taken aback.

"Do you remember two decades ago?" he said, seeming to change the subject. "I can never tell how old young people are…"

"I'm almost thirty," laughed Yuki. "Yeah, I remember. But what does that have to do with –"

"Yes, well, do you remember Narai's attempted attack on Scythia's eastern coast?"

"Of course…" she said, a lump forming in her throat. "That was when my father was killed."

"Then you know just how senseless it was. Some say that conflict triggered the one we're in now, or was at least used to galvanize the enemy against us."

"But this war is different," she said. "It's…"

"War is always the same," said Eiichi. "Be wary of what your command tells you."

Deciding not to pursue the current subject, she turned back to what she had last been looking at.

"The picture on the spine..." she said. "Is that shape..."

"Your stone? Yes, we each have one. It is our connection to Narajin."

"Yeah, but what does that..."

"Maybe another time you can read it and find out."

"Why not now?" she asked. "I thought these biographies could sort themselves."

"Yes, but tonight..."

He began to look distraught, as if trying to come up with a way to finish a sentence he knew he shouldn't have started. Abruptly, he turned and shuffled back towards his desk.

"Back to work," he muttered.

"Tonight is what?" she shouted after him, knowing full well that she wouldn't have gotten an answer even if Eiichi's faded hearing could pick up her voice.

As the evening wore on, she periodically walked past the row where she had found the book, thinking for a moment about attempting to get it and then deciding not to. Questions about what Eiichi had said about that night's importance burned in her mind as she went about her menial tasks.

When it finally came time to end her shift, she hurried out of the library as fast as she could and made her way towards the sleeping quarters. Changing into her night robe and throwing herself down on the mat, she let out and exasperated sigh, her mind still spinning with questions. There was still something strange about the denial surrounding Ken and the time he spent there.

Life in the temple was seemingly more comfortable than anything she had experienced in the military, but the feeling still nagged at her, something telling her there was more that needed to be done. It was what drove her to do what she did in the library, and what drove her to do what she knew she had to do tonight.

Chapter 3:
Altar of Narajin

The light streaming through the window gradually faded into soft gold and then disappeared. The other staff filed into the room and lay down, exhausted after their long day, occasionally throwing Yuki disdainful glances as she stared at the ceiling, pretending not to acknowledge them. There was no way of knowing whether they knew of her military connection if they hadn't seen her arrive, but it was reasonable to believe that word traveled fast through the community. It didn't matter, though. She had much more pressing questions to answer.

Hours passed and she felt herself periodically starting to drift off along with the rest of the room's occupants. Every time she jolted herself awake, and every time she tried to determine if now was the right time. After almost falling asleep for the fourth time in what seemed like as many minutes, she decided that if she didn't go now, she'd never get a chance again.

Silently as she could, she rose to her feet. Tiptoeing across the tatami mat, she stepped carefully over the sleeping denizens, trying to suppress the floorboards' urge to creak obnoxiously as she made her way to the screen that lead to the hallway. She slipped into her hall slippers and slowly nudged the screen to the side. With a deep breath, she stepped out. With the grace and stealth of a ghost, she glided to the stairs and started her descent of all fourteen flights to the ground floor. At each floor, she stopped briefly to make sure there was no activity. Her destination lay below – if the monks were having some kind of congregation, it would be in the ceremonial room at the base of the temple.

The normally open screen to the chamber, located at the back of the pagoda's first floor, was closed. The only light shining through its opaque textiles was moonlight that filtered in from the outside, giving the room a ghostly glow. Wondering if she had missed whatever happened, she slid the door open and entered, finding the chamber completely empty. The moonlight shined through the screens surrounding the room, softly illuminating the altar situated at the back, beyond the evenly spaced mattes upon which worshipers usually knelt.

There was no sign that any ceremony had taken place since that morning – the ornate altar, topped with a small red jade statue of Narajin, was still set exactly the same as it always was, with incense sticks on either side left unburned for the next day. Either they hadn't partaken in any kind of ceremony, or they had covered their tracks remarkably well.

Yuki was ready to leave and see if anything was happening outside, when she noticed something on the wooden floor just below the altar. One of the floorboards was slightly ajar from the rest, as if it had been pried up and left to sit there. Cautiously, she stepped closer to inspect it. Bending down and putting her fingers between the board and the rest of the floor, she pried it up with surprising ease. To her even greater surprise, there was nothing underneath it but a void of empty space. As far as she knew, the temple had no basement. This was something wholly unexplained, likely on the purpose of those who built and maintained it.

The void below was dark and quiet, but a faint sound echoed from below that told her something was down there. Putting the board to the side, she pried up the boards on either side with ease – they weren't even nailed down. As moonlight began to shine into the empty space before her, she started to make out stone steps beginning about three feet below the floor and continuing to spiral into the darkness.

An underground passage! Unbelievable.

Her face glowed with excitement at the discovery, surely the last thing she expected to find beneath a floor board – but it made perfect sense. No one knew the location of the Temple's secret ceremonial chambers except those at the highest level. If the monks had been through here, they had to be in whatever lay at the bottom of these stairs. Looking around to make sure she was alone, Yuki climbed into the stairwell, pulled the boards over the opening above her, and started down the steps into the unknown.

Slowly and carefully she descended through the darkness, gripping the cold stones in the wall and making sure her feet were landing on another step before shifting her weight. The last thing she wanted right now was to plunge into a bottomless abyss. Eventually, the murky blackness started to be driven out by a soft, fiery light from below. She could begin to hear the soft, slow beat of a drum, then as she spiraled closer, other instruments playing a traditional-sounding melody that she had never heard before. The music reverberated off the stone walls and ceiling, as if beckoning for her to continue.

The staircase was almost completely illuminated now, or at least her eyes had gotten used to low light. As she turned and descended one final spiral, the stairway opened into a wide hall and her feet touched down onto a solid stone floor.

Light from wall-mounted lanterns flickered along the cavernous hallway, making an otherwise terrifying environment feel warm and somewhat inviting. It appeared to be a tunnel, bored into the earth and reinforced, the surface smooth as polished marble. Still cautious, she followed the music that beckoned from the end, its melodies getting clearer and more vibrant as she drew closer to their source. She could smell incense burning, and could see moving shadows amidst the glow. Yuki thought she could hear the rhythmic footsteps of someone dancing.

To the left of the back wall, bathed in light, were two open doorways out of which Yuki couldn't see. They seemed to open into the same large space, as far as she could tell from the light and sounds emitting from them. Clinging to the wall, Yuki inched closer to the door before taking a deep breath to quell her fast-beating heart and peaked across the barrier.

Before her lay a vast cavern filled with lantern light. The monks stood with their backs to her, playing various instruments and facing some kind of altar, similar to the one upstairs in the Temple but much larger. In the middle of the altar sat a solid gold statue of Narajin, about a meter tall, similar to the one atop the front gate. This one had something around its neck – some kind of ornate, red jade pendant on a gold string.

Between the monks and the altar, a woman in a bright flowered kimono performed a beautiful ceremonial dance to the music with movements so fluid and mesmerizing that Yuki almost let out a gasp before stopping herself. It was the Priestess, and she was holding what appeared to be a stone like the one she had given Yuki, the one on the spine of that book in the library. Back and forth she danced, the music beginning to swell and gain momentum. The Priestess' movements quickened with the tempo, becoming more and more of a whirlwind without losing any of their grace.

Damn, Yuki thought, *she's in great shape.*

The beat of the drum pounded faster and faster, the music growing more intense, the dance seeming almost inhuman. Just when it seemed the musicians and the dancer were about to lose control, they abruptly stopped. The Priestess held her position in front of the altar, a deep bow below the statue with her hand holding the stone held upward towards it.

One of the monks, a tall and strapping young man, stepped forward towards the Priestess and knelt beside her. He took the stone from her hand and turned toward the statue of the lion god before bowing deeply. Slowly and assuredly, he reached for the amulet around the statue's neck and placed the stone in the center of it.

Yuki held her breath, waiting for something to happen. The monks stood motionless as the Priestess slowly looked up toward the amulet. Seconds passed. Nothing.

The monk holding the amulet took the stone out and inserted it again, as if this time it would have the desired effect. Still nothing. The other monks let out an audibly disappointed sigh as the Priestess rose to her feet, the enthusiasm of the dance having completely slipped away.

"Wait," commanded the young monk who had failed to accomplished whatever he had hoped to with the amulet, "why isn't it working?"

"We're still not worthy," another monk answered.

"We'll have to try again before the next military jerk shows up," said the Priestess, audibly frustrated.

This comment sent a jolt through Yuki's mind, seemingly a personal attack from the woman she thought she could trust.

"You mean that girl who arrived yesterday?" the second monk asked.

"No..." said the Priestess. "I like her. She's not like the last one."

Ken Sakurai. It didn't take long to realize that's who they were talking about. Had
he tried to do something that interfered with their ceremony?

"What if she finds out and reports back?" he asked

"She won't. Her intentions are in the right place – maybe even an alright choice, depending on what the god wants."

"Are you just saying that because –"

"Come on," said the Priestess, motioning toward the door. "I'm too tired to continue this right now."

As they began to turn to face the doorway, Yuki ducked to the side and hid against the wall. She didn't know what the punishment would be for being caught down here, but she was in enough trouble already. Looking around for someplace to hide, she saw a crevice at the bottom of the wall across from her just big enough for her to fit. Diving to the floor and climbing in, she hoped the shadows would obscure her presence.

The monks extinguished the lanterns in the cavern and filed out of the doorway one by one. Yuki watched their feet pass as she held her breath, hoping that she wouldn't be stuck when the time came to get out of her hiding place. The feet of the last person to leave were the Priestess'. They stopped for a moment next to Yuki's position, waiting a moment in silence. At last, she embarked down the hall, leaving only darkness behind her.

When she was sure they were out of earshot, Yuki exhaled and slid out into the hallway. The lanterns in the cavern had been blown out, but the embers still cast enough of a glow to see the basic outline of the altar. Curious about what she had just witnessed, she crossed the threshold and moved slowly towards the altar.

In the silence, she began to make out a sound that seemed to be coming from behind the wall of the chamber. It was faint, as if hundreds of feet of rock lay between her and its source, but it was a slow, deep, rhythmic rumbling that was unlike anything she had heard before. As she looked at the statue with the amulet around her neck, it dawned on her that she had heard something similar on the battlefield, although this was more subdued, less adrenaline-fueled and more peaceful – the breathing of a gargantuan creature deep in slumber.

Her heart raced faster than ever before. Everything started to fall into place – the purpose of the ceremony, what they were trying to accomplish. They were trying to wake Narajin. They *had* been trying to wake him, and yet they still weren't successful. The realization only raised more questions that she didn't expect to have answers to any time soon.

Surely they would try again, and maybe next time they could succeed in awakening the kaiju from its five thousand year slumber. Or would they? If the breathing told her one thing, it was that the god was still alive, and it was hibernating on the other side of the stone wall.

Realizing how tired she was, Yuki decided it was time for her to get some sleep herself. She now knew where this cavern was, and if she got a chance, she would come back and see the next ceremony. Maybe she would confront the Priestess about letting her join. Surely a woman that understanding would allow her to participate in such an event of such importance, and she seemed open to it from what she could decipher of the conversation.

Reaching into her pocket, she pulled out her stone that looked remarkably like the one used by the monk in the ceremony. She still had no idea what it was supposed to do, but it had something to do with the ornately carved red jade amulet hanging just above her on a thin gold chain around the neck of the statue. Looking up and examining the amulet, she saw that there was a smaller piece of dark green jade in the center, set with an imprint in the oval shape of the stone.

Without so much as thinking about what she was doing, she stretched her arm towards it, placing her stone in the gem just like the monk had. A bright light flashed before her eyes, and the room disappeared.

Chapter 4:

I Dreamt I Was a Giant

Darkness – thick and impenetrable, obscuring everything in Yuki's field of vision as she regained her other senses. It didn't take long to realize that she was buried, unable to move any part of her body from of the face-down position she was in. The amplified sound of her own breathing filled the claustrophobic tomb – deeper and heavier than usual, probably just the acoustics playing tricks on her. Her whole body felt strange, like she had just gone through rigorous training and all of her muscles were stiff and unresponsive. Even her head felt different. Strangest of all, there was something nagging in her mind, unfamiliar and trying to grab her attention away from the predicament she had found herself in, as if she were remembering something urgent but had no idea what it was.

Thinking back to her last memory in the ceremonial chamber, she wondered if the bright light she had seen had caused some kind of collapse in the cave, burying her deep below the surface and unlikely to be found. The thought terrified her – being entombed alive, fated to stay in this coffin-sized enclosure until she suffocated. As her heart rate increased, sweat worked its way out of her skin and into – *what was it?* To her horror, she felt a thick coat of hair covering body. With each new detail she discovered, the more it seemed like a horrible nightmare.

That's all this is, she began to tell herself, *right? A nightmare. Some kind of hallucination caused by temple magic.*

Usually once she figured out she was having a dream, she could force herself to wake up. This time, she only grew more and more conscious of how real every alien detail felt. She tried wiggling her leg, feeling the texture of the rock around it.

Yep, that's real.

As yet another surprise, the earth surrounding her gave way rather easily, dissolving like sand as she moved her leg through it. She could feel the small chamber shake slightly as the area by her foot caved in. Rather than a thousand tons of stone falling and crushing her, it felt more like a few buckets of dirt. She had to be close to the surface, which meant that she had been deliberately buried.

Overwhelmed by panic and fear, she tried to stand up. Her muscles flexed, lifting a much more robust body than she was used to. Even her proportions were different. She felt powerful. *Unnaturally* powerful. The earth above her rolled off her back and blinding sunlight pierced her eyes as she lifted herself out of the ground. Standing upright, the air of the outside world filled her lungs. After a few moments, her eyes began to adjust.

What...

Before her was a miniature version of the golden temple pagoda, probably about a meter tall – no, closer to a hundred and fifty centimeters, as it almost exactly matched her eye level. Around it was an exact scale replica of the blooming temple gardens, the red wooden gate, and beyond – the entire rest of the city. It had to have been created in painstaking detail, with every plant rendered in miniature form, every roof shingle in place, every structure a tiny, lifelike work of art. The wind gently rustled through the near-microscopic leaves on the trees as the sun shone down on the tops of the toy buildings at an angle suggesting that it was early morning in whatever this place was.

Yuki felt like her mind was on fire. She wanted to scream, or cry, or demand some kind of explanation for why the fabric of her reality was tearing itself to shreds.

Opening her mouth, she attempted to yell to anyone who could hear.

What the fuck is happening?!

Rather than a yell, the sound that came out of her was deafening, bellowing, and definitely not human. It echoed across the miniature city, causing a small shockwave that rustled the trees in the opposite direction of the wind. Windows on the pagoda started to open, and tiny heads poked out to look at her, their ant-like arms pointing and motioning frantically toward her as others joined them. The front gates opened and more insect-sized people rushed out into the garden. In the distance, inhabitants of the rest of the city made their way outside to see what was going on.

Yuki looked down at her hands – *claws.* Their long, blood red fur glistened in the sun, the sharp talons on her fingers extending and retracting as she opened and closed them. She felt the wind blowing through her mane, her fangs clamped together as she clenched her jaw. This was the moment for which the nation of Narai had waited five thousand years. It was the awakening of Narajin.

I'm... What?!

Unsure of what to do in what was undoubtedly the most unexpected situation in which she had ever found herself, she decided that the best course of action would be to lift her right leg and try moving forward in the general direction of the pagoda.

The ground cracked and reverberated with the immense impact of her footfall. People in the temple began to slowly retreat from the windows, some visibly cowering before the creature's advance. Narajin was a god, but he was also a monster of whom they actually knew nothing based on anything more than ancient myths. Little could they have known that the consciousness currently residing within him was that of a terrified woman still struggling to wrap her mind around inhabiting her new body.

Not wanting to accidentally hurt anyone, Yuki took several thundering steps away from the pagoda and toward the gate, pulverizing much of the flower garden in the process.

A few more steps and her shin went crashing through the gate, destroying the statue and sending shards of rubble flying in all directions. It didn't hurt, but it made her realize that collateral property damage was going to be an unfortunate side-effect of walking around town as a kaiju. She'd have to be careful not to accidentally smash any civilians, who would be difficult to spot scurrying underfoot.

Stomping down the road away from the temple, she found herself in the residential district of the city. Citizens poked their heads out of doorways to catch a glimpse of their freshly awakened deity, only to duck back inside out of fear. The vast majority of people alive had never seen a kaiju before, and something so massive was bound to inspire fear and wonder in whoever laid eyes upon it.

The proportions of Narajin's body were making it increasingly difficult for Yuki to control her basic motor skills. Her gait was a slow stumble, like a giant baby trying to maintain balance and avoid toppling over onto the homes of innocent people. While managing to keep from falling, she wasn't quite as successful in her attempts to avoid damage to the surrounding area – with every step she tore up sections of the road, and her inability to walk in a straight line meant that facades and front stoops were getting ripped and smashed off of houses and shops, revealing inhabitants inside. Still, to her knowledge she hadn't actually hurt anyone.

Then she heard a popping sound and felt a small, brief prick in the back of her left leg. Turning around as carefully as she could, she saw a tiny man standing in the middle of the street behind her holding a rifle and aiming it at her.

"Where were you?" he screamed in his barely audible voice, firing again. "You didn't help us! Now you're trashing our city? Monster?"

Yuki recognized that he was ex-military, too old to be a soldier but young enough to still have his strength. She felt terrible, because she knew exactly how he felt. If Narajin had been awake earlier, their battles against Scythia would have gone far differently – Commander Ito would probably still be alive, along with the countless others who had lost their lives in the rampage of Mokwa and Alkonoth.

Another pop sounded behind her, spurring her to turn back just in time for an explosive shell to strike her in the chest. A cannon sat atop an adjacent building, two men frantically loading it to fire again. Taking her by surprise and without time to think about operating her body, she lost balance and toppled forward onto the road, sending a shockwave through the ground and shaking the nearest buildings from their foundations.

Horrified, she pushed herself off the ground and rose to her feet, surveying the debacle around her. Dust hung in the air over the broken frames of houses as people climbed out of the wreckage, trying to clear the rubble away from the injured and move them to safety.

In the last few years, Narajin had become rather unpopular among those who thought he had been squandering his duty as the nation's protector. Now, compounded by her own inability to operate in the body of a giant behemoth, Yuki was feeling the full force of that resentment. As she stood motionless, trying to think of a way to avoid making things any worse, the presence in the back of Yuki's mind that had been bothering her like an oncoming migraine threw itself to the forefront until she could focus on nothing else. Her vision clouded, all other senses gradually fading as she felt her body making movements that were not of her control. She felt herself getting lighter as she left the corporeal body of the titan, entering a lucid disarray of white light.

Ok, she thought, *that was a dream, right? Am I waking up now? Am I dead?*

No, a deep, commanding voice seemed to say to her, *you are not dead, and that was not a dream. I needed to take control because you clearly have not prepared for this.*

What the hell is this, she demanded, *what's happening to me?*

We have combined, the voice said.

It was ancient-sounding, yet vital, and spoke directly to her thoughts.

Soon we will find a balance, it continued, *so that one of us does not have to take command like I have now.*

What? Yuki had no idea how to respond.

You have had no training prior to your first henshin. However, you are strong in mind and spirit – that is what I have been waiting for.

What are you talking about? Why am I here? Why was I... you?

The amulets, one of which you used to fuse with me, were created just before we entered our slumber. They were to allow each member of the Pantheon to share our consciousness with a human, so that we may better coexist with humanity and avoid the mistakes we made before. When you touched it, I looked into your mind. You are the first human I have deemed compatible.

I – I'm you now?

When you activate my amulet, wherever you are, your body will dematerialize and your consciousness will enter mine. We must learn to share control of our body if we are to fight together.

So... I'm not stuck here?

No. You may leave when you like.

Then get me the hell out of here. I didn't sign up for this, and I want my own body back.

32

In an instant, Yuki found herself looking up at the sky. She had a second to process that she was back in her old body before her back hit the ground with a thud, seemingly having materialized a meter or so in the air. She lay there motionless for a moment staring up at the clouds, trying unsuccessfully to absorb everything that had just happened. She felt like she had just awoken from a terrible dream that would hopefully slip away and be forgotten.

A powerful roar from Narajin, sitting a few meters to her left, let her know that it hadn't been a dream at all. She was in the company of her new companion, who looked down at her with visible disappointment.

"What?" she shouted, rising to her feet and facing him, "What do you want from me?"

The immense, vaguely humanoid lion sat in a catlike pose, looking back at her from far above, his feline eyes blinking and expressionless, showing a distinct lack of amusement. The creature was absolutely enormous, taking up her entire field of vision. She had been in the presence of Mokwa and Alkonoth in the chaos of battle, but getting a good look at a kaiju in broad daylight as it sat and stared at her was something else entirely.

He truly was a hundred meters tall when standing, and one of the claws on his fingers – the closest part to her – was bigger than her entire body. His appearance was surprisingly less like images of real lions that she had seen, and more like the stylized depictions of his own visage that she had always assumed were exaggerated, from the enlarged teeth and features of a guardian statue to the coloration and rounded face of a red lion dancer. His long, flowing fur covered his body completely, rather than in tufts and patches. Sitting down, he looked like a mountain.

Taking her eyes off the monster for a moment, she surveyed their location. They had perched on top of a foothill of the Kiso mountain range just outside the capital city, which she could see in the valley below, smoke rising from the path they had cleared in their rampage.

"So, you got us out of there," she spouted at the monster, half expecting it not to hear.

A reverberating grunt signaled that he had indeed heard her.

"At least that's over," she said in resigned disappointment at her utter failure to do whatever she was supposed to have done in the previous scenario. "Maybe you should've taken over sooner, 'cause I'm obviously no good at being you."

Narajin snorted, then lifted his left claw and scratched vigorously behind his ear. Dust and chunks of monster-sized dandruff fell on Yuki, prompting her to vocally express her displeasure and disgust. The gargantuan beast looked down and blinked at her with what almost looked like a smirk. Stretching out his limbs, he rolled onto his side with a cacophonous crash and sprawled out in the sun. Yuki had never had a cat, and this type of behavior was exactly what had always seemed off putting about them.

"So this is what the god of Narai acts like?" she said in the most condescending possible tone.

Barely opening one eye into a squint, he turned his head and looked at her. She could seemingly feel his gaze focusing on the amulet that still hung around her neck. With some hesitation, she reached up and put her hand around it, not quite knowing what would happen.

Now that we have joined, we can communicate whenever and wherever through the –

She quickly removed her hand from the amulet, cutting off the booming voice in her head mid-sentence, still not quite on board with sharing her mind with a giant monster. Narajin looked as displeased with her as ever.

"Look," Yuki retorted, "if you're not happy with getting me as a partner, or whatever this is, then... Well, I don't know. I didn't exactly choose to turn into a big stupid cat!"

As soon as the last remark had left her lips, Narajin rose to his feet, threw back his head, and let out a triumphant roar towards the heavens. Feeling slightly terrified, Yuki hesitantly reached up and touched the amulet again. As soon as her fingers made contact, Narajin's voice reverberated through her skull.

I am not a cat! I am a god!

Alright, alright! she thought back to him. *You're not a cat. We're really gonna have to work on that.*

She knew, unfortunately, that toning down a cat's god complex was near-impossible – especially one who actually was a god. On the bright side, she was getting the hang of speaking to him with her mind.

If we are to accomplish that for which I was awakened, he boomed, *we must gather the rest of the Pantheon Colossi.*

The other gods.

As far as Yuki knew, the nations of Avarta and Tarakona had been having as much luck as Narai in awakening their respective guardians, at least until she awakened Narajin herself. Fortunately for them, they weren't actively under attack by the enemy – but it was only a matter of time.

One still slumbers, one is missing, and two are under the influence of corrupt humans.

"Mokwa and Alkonoth," Yuki muttered, trailing off as images of the two giants crushing her army in battle came flooding back to her.

I've already met those two, she said.

Neither of them are evil – kaiju are a part of nature, and humans often abuse their relationship with the world they inhabit. It is possible that humans have pushed them to do things for their own personal gain.

That's when it struck her – that's why the Priestess didn't want the military interfering in the ceremony to awaken him.

Dammit Ken, she thought. *You really were a bastard.*

Who is Ken? The monster asked.

A total bastard.

Very descriptive.

He... Was that a snark?

I do not know what that means.

Exhaling heavily, she continued.

If other nations took control of their kaiju, it's possible that the Narai military wanted to do the same to you.

Silence on Narajin's end signaled that he was immensely troubled by this revelation.

I'm sorry, she said. *You helped us, and then some jerks planned to turn on you. I guess it's lucky that I showed up, right? Now we can find someone else who can do this whole thing better than I can.*

No, he said forcefully.

...To which part?

If you do not become my host, there is a chance that another like Ken will come along.

I'm not prepared, though. I'm not good at... whatever this is.

I am not prepared either, Yuki. This is a time of desperation for all of us. Do you not see what could happen if I am turned into a blunt instrument of war? Did you not see first hand where that would lead?

Flashes of the battlefield returned, Mokwa and Alkonoth's bloody rampage as vivid in her mind as ever.

You don't care? she said. *I don't think I'm the best person to be doing this.*

Your words, said Narajin. *Not mine.*

Wow, okay. Why do you need me at all?

Because I cannot do this on my own. You are a willful, compassionate spirit. You have what the Pantheon Colossi needs to end this malice before it is too late.

...Thanks.

In addition, finding another host would be too time consuming. We must move quickly.

Now that sounds more genuine. I just don't know about...

She nearly finished the sentence before thinking about what it entailed. Going back to the military empty-handed and facing a court martial would be going back to certain doom. This, at least, would give her an opportunity to... be a daikaiju. The more she thought about it, the more she realized that this was the only chance she had to keep the people she cared about safe. Maybe that was what the Priestess meant when she said she might be "an alright choice."

Well, what about the other two? she said. *Still snoozing their lives away like you were?*

Narajin didn't look amused by the jab.

My brother Ganejin still waits in Avarta for a compatible human to join with him. Jhalaragon is a free spirit – it is possible that he has a host, but I cannot know for certain until we go to meet him.

Not much help we can be in that area, is there.

On the contrary... There may very well be humans like yourself who simply do not know what they are meant to do.

It can't be easy to find them. What, do we go through the entire population until we see somebody who fits? I can't imagine anyone will be too receptive to some foreign girl and a giant ca– uh, you know, telling them it's their destiny to turn into a monster.

I can talk to my brother when we reach him. The answer may be closer than you'd think. It wasn't for a lack of brave humans that made me wait for you, just that none of them used the amulet.

Wow, thanks. That's the plan, then? Find Ganejin and Jhalaragon and just tell them we're getting the gang back together?

Narajin nodded his head once. Yuki began to feel more enticed by this scenario than she had been before. Something was stirring within her, a sense of purpose to her strange debacle. If she was going to be stuck sharing her consciousness with a monster, she was going make the most of it.

Well, it's not like I have anything going on here. I guess we're going to Avarta.

The great lion began to shift from side to side in what almost appeared to be excitement. He let out a growl of approval as Yuki held her stone up to the amulet and prepared for the rush of the henshin.

Time to wake up some gods.

Chapter 5:
Scorch Marks of Atom Fire

We will never get anywhere if you do not clear your mind.

With Narajin's voice booming through her – *their* – head, Yuki tried again. She could feel the presence of his consciousness telling her to lift their right leg first, which she did as they stumbled forward another step.

Still late on response, he critiqued, *but we are getting better.*

They had somehow made it out of the mountains in the last hour or so without falling off of any cliffs, and were now slowly but surely making their way to the coast across the wildflower sprinkled hills of eastern Narai, the noonday sun illuminating their blood red fur in all its glory. Yuki was sure that people were watching them – sure to keep their distance after the incident in the city had proven how unstable they were. It was still strange to think that she was now part of a widely-talked-about spectacle and possibly the most significant event to happen in the country in centuries. It hadn't fully sunk in, not that she was sure it ever could.

They would have to cross the narrow western sea and then travel across the dead lands to reach the nation of Avarta, which meant learning how to swim when she barely had a grasp on walking. Narajin was supposedly a good swimmer, a strange ability for a cat.

You do not actually have to learn how to swim, Narajin interjected, clearly picking up on her thoughts. *You only have to access the part of our mind that already knows. We have many abilities that must come to us through mental discipline! And I am not a cat.*

Yuki had her own ways of clearing her mind of thought – it was something she had to do to preserve some semblance of mental stability after having been in combat. That was one thing, though. Getting used to sharing her mind with a giant cat – *Yeah, that's right, cat!* – was something else entirely. She was, however, beginning to get better at sensing his motor signals and responding in time with her own to get their lumbering body to take one step after another.

The more they focused on the task at hand, the more Yuki realized that it wasn't entirely different from what she had done with the Priestess in the garden only the day before. It wasn't just distraction, it was giving purpose to her thoughts and actions. If this was how easy it was, then how could it be that much harder to swim? To fly?

No, Yuki, we cannot fly.

Dammit.

Through the unfamiliar, giant eyes of the lion god, Yuki was grateful for any chance she had to watch the beautiful countryside pass them by from her towering perspective – green rolling hills and a roaring river flowing towards the sea. It was a different way of looking at Narai than she was used to, but the kaiju's eye view was not a bad one.

There are abilities you have, Narajin continued, *that I may learn as well.*

Yeah, she said. *I could show you some moves if we get in a fight.*

You take pride in fighting.

I'm good at it.

The silence that followed on Narajin's end could either have signaled approval or concern, but at that point she couldn't be bothered to ask.

Even at the uneven, leisurely pace at which they strode towards the sea, they were covering such an immense distance with every step that it would probably take them only about an hour to traverse the hundred kilometers. One positive to the new body was that it had incredible stamina – she hadn't felt physically tired at any point since fusing with the monster.

What do you eat? she asked, getting increasingly good at directing her thoughts toward Narajin, even if he could read all of her thoughts anyway.

We do not, normally...

Wait, that's bullshit. I've heard that kaiju used to eat people.

Kaiju run on mana, the energy of the Earth. All living things contain this energy, so a kaiju can gain sustenance by eating other creatures, but only if absolutely necessary. It is not something I particularly enjoy at this point in my life.

So how do you get it?

The Sun. Water. Molten lava has a high concentration of mana.

You eat lava?

When I can get to it, yes.

I bet that's great for your taste buds.

It is delicious, actually.

She couldn't imagine what eating lava would be like, and didn't really want to find out. Narajin would have to do that on his own time. Another question formed in her mind, and she didn't have to wait for an answer.

Our bond itself creates mana as well. The bond between two or more beings coming together for something greater than themselves is one of the greatest sources of energy in the universe. That is how I was awakened after so long.

Yuki could hardly believe what she was hearing.

I'm not even sure if I like you! she spat.

You have great compassion within you, Yuki. That is why you seek to defend others and honor the legacy of your father.

At this point the discussion was getting a far too personal. Rather than dig deeper into the mess of metaphysical mumbo jumbo he would no doubt continue to spout, she cleared her mind and focused entirely on perfecting the art of walking. With any luck, they'd get to the coast by noon with enough time to figure out how to swim another four hundred kilometers before dark.

Swimming was in fact easier than she had anticipated once she honed in on Narajin's thoughts and followed his motions in much the same manner that they had learned to walk together. As they paddled away from the shore, she turned around to give one last look back at the serene shore of her homeland. There was no way to know the next time she would see its green hills and saturated skies. She had never left Narai in her life, and here she was swimming away on the first step in her journey toward the distant land of Avarta - a country with whom only sea traders of Narai had passing encounters, given the distance and what lay between them.

The sky had begun to fade into a soft gold when the setting sun touched the horizon before them and revealed the first glimpses of the shore. Immense, shadowy structures loomed like mangled mountains silhouetted by the dying light. The dead lands were vast, stretching from the coast of the Narai sea to the borders of Avarta five thousand kilometers to the west, and as far north as the Scythian Empire.

The outlines before them stretched kilometers upward into the clouds and covered the horizon, even with parts of them missing or toppled over. Yuki would've thought that they were a mountain range, if not for their inorganic shapes that alternated between perfectly linear and horribly mangled, sharp, complex geometries that jutted out at every angle.

As they neared the shore, the shapes became visible in all their eerie majesty. Yuki was awestruck by the sight of the weathered monoliths as they climbed out of the water and walked down what seemed to have once been a giant highway, the technological giants of the past looming on either side. They were like mountains of incorruptible metal, filled with the ruins of incomprehensible machines that were obviously man-made but far beyond anything the current world was capable of engineering. It likely had once been a city in some time before recorded history began – before the great fire, and the first kaiju war. Now they stood lording over an inhospitable wasteland, impossible relics of a forgotten age.

Darkness setting in, they stopped in the shadow of a ruined monolith that looked almost like a giant sword, piercing upwards into the sky. Its top had been shattered, its sides weathered by time, but it still looked like nothing Yuki had ever seen.

There is no way to maintain our energy here unless we rest, said Narajin. *Perhaps we should stop for the night.*

Light flashed before Yuki's eyes as she separated from Narajin and fell onto the ground, mentally exhausted but relieved to be back in her own body. She lay on her back and stretched out, her eyes and thoughts still occupied by the eeriness and majesty of her surroundings.

The ground was littered with broken pieces of rock and metal, marked by having been charred in some kind of intense heat. It wasn't exactly comfortable to sit on, but there wasn't much of a choice for accommodations. The air was thick with a kind of damp mist, probably a combination of the nearby ocean air and the chilled wind that funneled through the ruins. It was cold, especially for summer, but Yuki didn't mind lower temperatures as long as they weren't freezing.

How could these people have just disappeared? she thought, half to herself and half to her companion.

There was a time long ago, Narajin said heavily, *before even I existed, when humans set fire to the Earth.*

The great fire, said Yuki. *The legend. We all heard it as children.*

The atom fire, he continued. *It shattered continents and made this land toxic and unlivable. It was that fire that brought forth the kaiju.*

Weren't there kaiju before that? she asked.

There have always been great beings of the Earth... Of those I know, only Mokwa remembers the time before the fire. She was born of the ice age in eons past, and walked among the first humans when they still lived in harmony with nature. She entered a long sleep just as humanity was beginning to wake up to its potential. The fire came much later... and it brought the destroyers.

Then you guys came from... the atom fire, Yuki said, piecing together remembered parts of myth and Narajin's recited memory.

When my brother Ganejin and I were spat into this world, he continued, *the wounds of the Earth were so great that new monsters emerged. Our only thought or purpose was to annihilate humanity so that life may begin anew, and we would have succeeded if Mokwa had not arisen from her slumber. She knew humans better than any of us, as she had seen them live in balance with the world. We had not. We three were joined by Alkonoth and Jhalaragon soon after, and together defeated the destroyers. Humanity dubbed the five of us the Pantheon Colossi and took us as their gods. The amulets were meant to ensure that such a catastrophe never again occurred, so that we may fight together with humans in defense of the world we helped rebuild.*

The flood of revelations washed over Yuki. She had heard stories of the Pantheon's war against the destroyers as a child, but that the saviors had been among the enemy had not been part of it. Narai didn't have the best track record with teaching their past, but this extended far beyond. Moreover, the true nature of her companion was now in question.

You were a destroyer, she replied. *You... killed humans?*

We were all... Narajin's voice hung low in shame as he struggled to find the words. *It was a different time. We did not know humanity like we do now. Humans had caused so much damage that we couldn't see the good through the bad. If only –*

How many people did you kill?

Yuki's question hung in their minds. She could sense that Narajin was struggling with the answer, but all that came from his side was silence.

"How many people did you kill?!" Yuki yelled aloud, her voice echoing through the ghostly man-made canyons. At last the great lion responded.

When Mokwa found us, we had all but completed our task.

Your "task"? Who sent you?

We were created by the mistakes of the old civilization, born of the atom fire.

So you just took it upon yourselves to... Do you have any idea how that sounds? I thought "monster" was just talking about your size, but I'm starting to think it means something else. And this is the great god who helped build Narai, after almost wiping us off the face of the planet?

Yuki... There are no excuses for what we did. I am telling you this so that we may acknowledge that what we did in the past was wrong. Humans and kaiju have both committed horrible acts to the planet and to each other. The time before the Pantheon Colossi and the building of the five nations was a period of history that must never be repeated. The Earth still has not fully recovered... Just look around you.

The charred ruins of the ancient world stared back at them like specters of the billions dead at the hands of humans and kaiju alike. The wrongs committed in war were all too familiar to Yuki, but this conflict had been on another scale entirely. She brushed her fingers against the ground, picking up a handful of gravel and metal shards before letting them go.

I still don't know what you assholes thought gave you the go ahead to do that, she spat back. *Maybe you should've just let us destroy this shitty planet on our own accord. Look, I'm sorry for my ancestors creating you with their atom thing, but you still killed innocents.*

I will never try to justify or distance myself from those horrific events, Narajin continued, still carrying the immense weight of shame in his voice. *It was a time when we knew far less. The rest of the Pantheon feel the same way. That is why we turned on the others. The destroyers who did not defect with us had blinded themselves. Mokwa has the least amount of blood on her hands, as she showed us that humans are truly gentle, compassionate creatures when they allow themselves to be. Perhaps that is why she has fallen under the influence of bad humans now. She is trusting of your kind in the purest way, as she lived amongst them when they were in their infancy. She showed us the greatness of humans when all we had seen was their worst.*

He turned and looked at Yuki with eyes filled with sadness and remorse. They shared a moment of silence, the barrier of resentment in front of Yuki beginning to melt as she felt the pain of the giant creature's responsibility for his mistakes. At last he continued.

All living things who have not lost their way simply desire to live, to have companionship, and to make the most of the time that they have. The wrongs of the past were not erased when that truth was imparted to me, but I did learn a valuable lesson about why we were wrong. Why it must never be allowed to happen again.

Looking into his eyes, she could feel the urge for tears to begin welling up in her own, though she fought them back. The discussion could not have come at a more opportune time – she had just come face to face with the fact that the organization to which she had pledged herself had planned to commit a crime against the being in front of her, and likely to the entire planet. There had to be a way to stop this conflict, before something like this happened again. If the kaiju could face the mistakes of their kind, then so could she.

Narajin and Yuki spent the rest of the night looking up at the stars that shone brightly through the tops of the metal canyons. The same stars had covered the night sky at the time of the great annihilation, but the beings underneath them had changed irrevocably. Though their kind had once been mortal enemies, a kaiju and a human now shared an understanding that extended far beyond a tenuous alliance. They had emerged from the horrors of the past, and against all odds, they were friends.

Chapter 6:

Warrior's Mercy

The term "dead lands" was more accurate than Yuki had hoped. Beyond the city lay an endless, scorched desert across which rumbled a relentless, cold wind that pierced to the bones of even Narajin. Shards of the sharp, jagged ground dug into their feet, having been petrified to a charred scab on the Earth's mortal wound. The atomic fires of times long past had left little in their wake. The landscape looked much as it might have in the planet's infancy, when the molten rock was newly cooled and life had yet to appear. Yuki hated this place.

I hate this place.

I know, Narajin responded, *you have been thinking about how much you hate it since we got here.*

Why couldn't we have gone to the south?

It was a fair question on Yuki's part. The stretch of obliterated wasteland between Scythia and the lush southern wilds of the mainland Asian continent was notoriously one of the most inhospitable pieces of land on Earth.

Traveling fast as possible is far more important than taking a scenic route, said Narajin.

Yeah, well, it'd be nice to see something besides burnt rocks and grey clouds.

She could sense Narajin's worry about the last point – it had been days since they had encountered the last spot of sunlight for him to stop and soak up. Even then, he was reluctant to let her separate from him, for fear that she would be harmed by the harsh conditions. Braving the wasteland in the body of a kaiju was bad enough, but fifteen minutes in a human body had been almost unbearable.

I still have plenty of strength left, he assured her, although his tone signaled that he wasn't entirely convinced himself.

They still had about a week of travel at their current pace before reaching Avarta, and if they didn't hit sunlight, or miraculously find a lake, there was a distinct possibility that they wouldn't make it. Of course there were other sources of mana, but the likelihood of finding an erupting volcano or having a sudden burst of mutual inspiration in this environment was even less.

The barren, scorched landscape and the previous day's conversation left another thought hanging in Yuki's mind.

What happened to all the people who lived here? Did they all die?

No... The land was made uninhabitable by the war, but many persevered. Much of Narai is descended from refugees from these lands, and those to the south.

The revelation made Yuki feel slightly better, if still revolted at the thought of so much human life being lost. It did strengthen her opinion of her home, built by survivors rather than those who closed themselves off and hid while the world died.

So, do you think my ancestors lived here? she asked.

Undoubtedly.

As the trek continued, Yuki began to notice something in the distance, just to the north. She couldn't quite make out what it was, but it looked like several small specks that had been moving gradually across the bleak horizon toward the southwest.

Yes, Narajin acknowledged, *I see it too.*

What is it? Yuki inquired.

I am not sure. It could be humans, but it does not seem like a trade envoy – and its point of origin is in the north, which means it is coming from Scythia.

Then it dawned on Yuki, and a wave of fear washed over her.

It could be a scouting party, she said. *That means the Scythians are planning to attack Avarta. But that doesn't make sense... Mokwa and Alkonoth are on the north island of Narai with the Scythian army.*

Yes, Narajin responded, sounding just as worried as Yuki felt, *but the attack on Narai could be a diversion for a two-pronged invasion in the south.*

Yuki had wondered why the enemy forces hadn't advanced after their victory over the Narai army, and had stayed on the northern island. It certainly made sense – Avarta had a small standing army, but Tarakona was completely pacifistic. Both countries would be considerably easier to take if the army of Narai was occupied. If those two nations fell, there would be no way to stop the enemy from controlling all of civilization.

But what about the monsters, Yuki wondered. *Will they stay behind while the armies invade?*

There are several dormant volcanos on the north island of Narai. It is possible that the enemy plans to cause an eruption that would allow Mokwa and Alkonoth to enter a volcano and swim through the Earth's mantle to Avarta or Tarakona.

Holy crap.

It is likely to happen.

The specks on the horizon gradually shifted their course away from them – there was no doubt they had noticed the kaiju lumbering across the desert. Yuki and Narajin didn't even have to ask each other how they wanted to respond. With a sudden burst of energy, they broke into a sprint, then dropped to all fours and began bounding across the terrain toward the receding enemy battalion.

If Narajin's normal walking speed was impressive, Yuki didn't know what to call what she was experiencing. Wind howled past their ears and the atmosphere seemed to part before them as they galloped after the enemy that scurried away from them like insects. The Scythian troops began to come into closer view and Yuki could see their shock trooper armor and long-range rifles – they had no doubt been on their way to raid some helpless village and take whatever they could before heading back across the desert to wherever their camp was located. Their bulky armor covered them like a beetle's exoskeleton, expanding their imposing silhouettes to frighten any civilians they might encounter into submission.

In one swift motion, Yuki and Narajin dove in front of them, blocking their trajectory with a crouching stance and hissing forcefully, blowing some of them backward off their feet.

We will not kill them, Narajin reminded her, *just send them back to where they-*

Nope, too bad.

Yuki focused all of her mental strength toward their left hand, which she lifted into striking position over a group of roughly thirty cowering soldiers.

Yuki, no!

With all the force she could muster, she smashed their palm into the ground. A tremendous boom resounded from the impact, echoing across the desert as pieces of debris flew into the air and rained down.

Narajin yanked back control as they rose to their feet. A claw-shaped crater lay in front of them. At the bottom of it, embedded in the earth, were a swath of red smears and scattered carnal pulp amidst the flattened remains of armored uniforms. Pulverized pieces of bone and shreds of musculature lay strewn meters from bodies that had been dismembered by the force of impact. Turning to the north, the living members of the battalion fled like terrified prey from the wrathful kaiju.

Yuki felt exhilarated – the Scythians would think twice about trying to attack Avarta. At long last, she had been able to accomplish something in this meaningless conflict. The sensation washed over her, a wave of satisfaction at having delivered brutal retribution upon those whom she'd normally have feared. Unfortunately, her moment of glory was soon cut short.

You cannot kill like that! Narajin seethed. *You, more than anyone should understand that they are just soldiers.*

Oh, come on! If we didn't stop them, they were gonna kill innocent people. That's what they do.

What you did to them was an execution. You must remember that when you are with me, you are a daikaiju. You cannot massacre humans. Compared to them, your power is insurmountable.

So, what, she spat incredulously, *we let them go?*

We let them live. Do you think they would have returned after coming face to face with a kaiju?

She looked at the spot on the ground where the tiny red smears marked the final resting places of the Scythian troopers. It was a horrible sight, but so was all war. Maybe they would've changed if she had only scared them away. She had been a soldier herself, even though she didn't agree with the former imperialism of her own country.

Well it's not my fault for what they were doing, she bit back.

A sickening feeling clawed at her insides.

Fine, she continued, not wanting to deal with further criticism. *I went too far. Leave it at that. You don't have any high ground here.*

In silence, they turned to the southwest, the setting sun that had finally managing to glimmer through the clouds ahead of them.

It was a mistake. Narajin still sounded upset, but slightly more understanding than before. *War manages to put innocent blood on all of our hands sooner or later.*

Through her contemplation of whether or not she actually agreed with Narajin's lesson, Yuki began to lose track of the days and nights that they traveled through the inhospitable cold and acidic rain. Thoughts of the value of the lives she had taken, and of the horrible devastation that was yet to occur overwhelmed her, but still they trekked on.

As they continued, the ground began to grow softer and the skies began to clear. Golden sunlight shone through the clouds more often and plant life began to emerge from the dirt. The land of Avarta was much closer in proximity to the dead lands than Narai, but its lush topography was at least as beautiful.

Trees came into view, first one by one, then expanding into a vast green jungle ahead of them. Sounds from a myriad of creatures running and swinging through the vegetation echoed around the monster's feet. A flock of scaly, featherless birds with horned crests flew at Narajin's eye level. Looking down, Yuki could see the tiny forms of monkeys moving swiftly through the canopy. One of them looked up and made eye contact, its face the image of a bony, external skull.

Abnormalities from mutation, said Narajin.

They look like they're doing fine, all things considered, Yuki responded.

They are. These animals have adapted. It was not always the case, though. Countless species were driven extinct in –

Alright, I misspoke, she cut him off, deciding that there had been enough depressing revelations for one week.

Beyond the trees rose the shapes of tall structures, gleaming in the sunlight. The Palaces of Avarta were marvels of human engineering. Thousands of years old and taller than kaiju at more than three hundred meters each, adorned with ornate decorations and iconography of the Pantheon and Avarta's magnificent animals alike, and awash in a dazzling array of all the primary colors, they greeted visitors to the realm with their humbling, intense beauty.

People began to poke their heads out from the buildings across the city as Narajin drew closer, wide-eyed and unbelieving at the towering behemoth as it continued its advent down the main road. Though they would be understandably hesitant at the arrival of another nation's guardian monster in their city, Yuki certainly enjoyed these people's reception more than the one they had received in Narai.

Well, she thought, *it doesn't look like they're gonna attack us.*

If only they knew why we were here, Narajin replied. *Awakening my brother will be... an ordeal for all of us.*

Yeah, what's that going to entail again?

As far as I can discern, he does not yet have a human with whom to join. If we wake him without the preparation of his people, he will be at his most animalistic.

Yuki felt a pit in her stomach began to form.

Uh, so what is he going to do?

We will have to contain him.

Sensing apprehension from his end, Yuki resisted the urge to make a snarky response. They had a huge task ahead of them. In the mean time, the overwhelming feeling coming from Narajin was almost euphoric. He probably hadn't seen Avarta since the founding of the five nations, and in the millennia since it had been built into a wondrous civilization.

Citizens lined the streets to see the lion kaiju. Yuki and Narajin took special care to keep centered on the road so as not to accidentally flatten a spectator. Yuki wasn't sure she had seen this many people in one place in her life – the bright colors of their clothing created a rainbow sea that stretched for miles in all directions.

Narajin ground their walk to an abrupt halt. About to ask what the problem was, Yuki noticed that there was a line of people standing shoulder to shoulder across middle of the road, wearing ceremonial-looking military uniforms. In the center, just in front of the rest, stood a man draped in luxurious robes and topped by a bright purple headpiece with an ornate gold crest mounted on the front.

I think it might be time for me to disembark, Yuki told her companion, *I can do the talking.*

A flash of light and a brief fall later, and Yuki felt the full impact of the road rising up to hit her. She was now flat on her face, just in front of the man who she assumed was a ruler. The crowd went silent, save for quiet gasps and a few stifled laughs. It must have been strange, she imagined, to see a foreign girl materialize out of thin air and plop face down into the dirt in front of them. Slowly she rose to her feet and looked around at the astonished faces. It didn't take long to realize that her face was covered in mud, which she quickly tried to wipe off to no avail. The king was the first to speak.

"I presume that you are an avatar of the god Narajin," he said in a deep, stately voice.

"An avatar..." she responded, not entirely sure how to address a king, "Yeah, that sounds about right. I'm Yuki, your... excellency?"

He stared at her for a long second before his serious composure burst into a good-natured laugh. Her expression still frozen in embarrassed shock, Yuki's eyes darted from the man to his armed escort to the crowd around them, unsure of how to interpret his reaction. At last he managed to calm himself down and took a deep breath before responding.

"I am Bhagavat-Deva the Seventh, Maharaja of this nation. Please accept my welcome, Yuki, to Avarta."

Forcing a smile in return, she tried to mouth "thanks," but was too on-edge to make sounds come out. The Maharaja lifted a finger pointing upwards at her monstrous companion and opened his mouth as if formulating his next phrase before continuing.

"Tell me," he said, still smiling but his eyes taking on a look that showed he was ready to talk business, "what brings a kaiju here – for the first time, I might add, since the founding of this country? Not a very common sight, to say the least."

She wasn't sure if cutting to the chase was the best course of action in this discussion, but she decided to do it anyway.

"We've come to wake up Ganejin."

The king's face turned far more serious as soon as the words had escaped her mouth.

"Ganejin has rested for five thousand years," he began, "and he shows no signs of rising today. We must perform the correct rituals to gain his trust and attention. It will take months to get the ceremonies in place. Not to mention that the scriptures state that it is only in a time of great need that he be woken."

"You misunderstand," she interjected, "we need him immediately. Avarta is in great danger, as is the entire world. If Ganejin is not awakened, the armies of Scythia and Laurentia will sweep across the southern nations."

"I have heard that the armies of Scythia are stretched thin in their war against Narai," he said, his eyes narrowing incredulously, "a war, I might add, that has become a terrible stalemate. Their government crumbles from unrest, their people revolt, and their alliance with a country on the other side of the planet grows tenuous – it is my job, after all, to know these things. They can't even take the nation next to them, so how will they march across the dead lands and take Avarta?"

"Their alliance with Laurentia is built on one thing," said Yuki. "They have the help of two kaiju. The rumors of Alkonoth and Mokwa's resurrection are true. I've seen them in battle myself."

"But Laurentia is on the far side of the world, and their borders remain isolated. If they attempted an invasion by sea, Tarakona would stand between them and us."

"Are you just ignoring the fact that they have kaiju helping them?"

"The kaiju are not our concern... yet. I do see your point in coming, and I see what you are trying to do, but my job as a leader is to weigh the options and determine what is best for my people, and right now, unleashing the power of Ganejin – unrestrained – seems like the worse scenario by my judgment."

The king scowled and turned around to face his advisors, who leaned in to whisper to him. Starting to panic, Yuki grabbed her amulet to contact Narajin.

This whole thing is going south real fast.

Just wait, he assured her.

After a few nerve-wracking moments, the Maharaja turned to face her.

"Seeing as you are a kaiju," he said, sounding somewhat defeated, "there is no way we can stop you from doing what you came here to do. But please heed my warning that the great Ganejin will not be easy to reason with. As a member of the Pantheon, it is your duty to stop him from bringing death and destruction to us all."

"You have my word," Yuki told him, speaking with the full gravitas of the situation, "and the word of Narajin."

With that, she inserted her stone into the amulet and vanished back into the kaiju.

I can't guarantee that we will be able to stop him, Narajin said upon her arrival.

Well then, we've gotta do everything we can.

Continuing their advent down the main road as the crowd parted in front of them, Yuki looked out at the ocean of reveling people. Their welcoming attitude had not been diminished by their ruler's apprehension, whether it be through disagreement or lack of knowing of his worries.

Do you think it would be wrong to... I dunno, stop and take advantage of these people's hospitality? Yuki asked.

We must make haste, said Narajin. *Besides, I would not fit in any of their houses.*

I would. If the world ends tomorrow, don't you think I deserve to... party with some other cool girls?

Yuki's gaze drifted down to a group of women in vivid, ornate outfits of flowing, light fabrics. It was a fabulous look, she thought. Discussing fashion points and, maybe, finding another woman with similar inclinations to her own would be a welcome distraction from the carnage that both awaited her and trailed in her wake.

I do not understand that concept, said the kaiju, nonplussed.

What, a party?

I have never heard of it.

Oh, man, it's... Well, it's like a big explosion of excitement.

A party is an explosion?

You know what, never mind.

Ganejin's main temple, the location of his hibernation chamber, was still one thousand kilometers from the city. She knew that Narajin would have to keep moving through the night to reach it, but there was still something she wanted to try.

I can henshin into you from anywhere, she said. *Right?*

That is correct.

Then wherever you are, I just... zap right into you and I'm there. Right?

What are you suggesting?

You keep moving, cover as much ground as you need to, and then I join up with you tomorrow before you get there. It's not like I'd be doing much of anything besides tagging along anyway.

Narajin paused for a moment, as if considering her request. It was true that he could cover most of the journey on his own and then she could join him later.

What if I run into obstacles? he asked. *I may need your help.*

I seriously doubt there'll be anything you can't handle without me before we get to your brother, she said, hoping that he would at least allow her a little leeway – it would make all the difference in their friendship to know that she wasn't just his human pawn.

Very well, he conceded, *but please be sure to return before I reach the temple tomorrow. I cannot partake in your human activities, but I wish for you to have a good time.*

Aww, she vocalized at the monster's show of affection. *I'll just have to have twice as much fun in your honor.*

Please do not cause any expl–

Relax! I'm not gonna party that hard.

A chill ran through her as images from the last few days appeared from memory. She ignored them and disembarked.

Chapter 7:
Gift from the Gods

Gentle wind blew through the red silk drapery to the other side of the room where it rattled a curtain of red, decorative beads that hung over the doorway. The light of early morning shone through the curtains, letting Yuki know that it was time to awaken, despite the disorientating sensation in her head telling her otherwise. A night of combat and a night of revery often had a similar physical toll on her body, but the scene to which she awoke after the latter was vastly preferable.

"Hell of an explosion," she muttered to herself before immediately wincing at the joke's poor taste.

Narajin's utter confusion at such a basic human concept truly highlighted how different he was despite all efforts to bridge the gap. There would be things he would never be able to understand, but at least he was making an effort. Still, it amused her that for a being of immense power with seemingly mystical knowledge of the universe, he was utterly clueless to the details of human behavior.

Thinking about him made her realize that she needed to check in to see where he was. If he had traveled through the night, he would likely be reaching the Temple of Ganejin around noon – fortunately still a ways off.

A soft groan to her right interrupted her thoughts. The feminine hand that had been resting on her stomach under the sheets lifted and moved to the left side of her body where it landed, caressing her gently.

Turning to her right, she saw the face of the still sleeping woman she had met the night before resting on the pillow next to her – a welcome sight for one of the first images Yuki had seen that day. The woman had a darker complexion and sharp features – seemingly in her late twenties, though she could've been slightly younger. Her long, black hair almost reminded her of the Priestess', if a bit fuller. This thought immediately struck Yuki as strange, that she would think of the woman she had left behind in Narai while taking in the glorious sight of the totally different one she was with. Was there an emotional attachment? She wouldn't even have time to consider it with her journey taking her further and further away. Responsibility came first.

The last night had been wild, exhilarating, and everything one could have hoped for in a celebration for the arrival of a Pantheon host in a nation that didn't seem to despise them yet. Moreover, it had been an extremely necessary distraction from the war. Best of all, of course, had been the woman who was now sleeping next to her.

Upon meeting she had seemed so sure of herself, so confident in approaching Yuki – something that appealed to her far more than a groupie who just wanted the thrill of being with the host of a kaiju with no regard for her as a human. Maybe that was part of it, but at least she had been interested in Yuki in other ways. With their encounter playing out to its fullest possible extent, it had been a fantastic night – something to which the condition of the sheets could attest.

Opening her eyes, the woman smiled at Yuki as her hand gave her a gentle massage.

"Good morning," Yuki laughed slyly.

The woman smiled back, sliding her right leg over Yuki's body until she was nearly straddling her. Considerably taller than Yuki, her legs reached much further down the length of the bed.

"Don't you have somewhere to be?" asked her companion.

"Yeah..." she exhaled. "Not right away."

"Oh. I do," said the woman, pulling her hand away. "Sorry."

This was surprising, as it was the first time in a while that Yuki had even thought about the continuing goings on in people's normal, day to day lives.

"Are you sure?" said Yuki, perhaps in an effort to entice the woman into staying.

It had occurred to her during the night that if Yuki could find a host for Ganejin in this crowd of people, the coming ordeal would be much less difficult. Unfortunately, revelers were not the most reliable pool from which to draw a dedicated warrior.

"Yeah, I'm sorry," the woman said, planting a slow kiss on Yuki's lips before drawing back and slipping out from under the covers to pick up her clothes from the previous night off the floor.

"Do you..." Yuki began, trying to think of a way to phrase the question before, as usual, diving right in. "Do you want to come with me?"

The woman turned slowly and looked at her, an incredulous look on her face, before bursting out laughing.

"I'm serious!" said Yuki. "Ganejin needs a host. We need to find –"

"Someone..." said the woman. "Not me. I'm not gonna fight. Besides, I need to stay here. I've got... You know, a life. A career."

Yuki sat for a moment, letting the words sink in. She was a fighter, but many weren't. The woman before her seemed to be strong willed and dedicated, qualities that would be necessary in a host for the Pantheon – but in a different way.

"I figured it was worth a shot," she said. "I'm sorry."

"No," said the woman as she hastily dressed herself. "I understand. I know how important it is, it's just... not me."

"You sure you don't want to learn how to fight? I could teach you."

"It's not my life. Not everyone can just give up everything they have and go off with a monster. Even if I wanted to. I'm honestly amazed that you did it."

"So am I," said Yuki, looking down and smiling to cover the intense confusion she felt. "I'm amazed that people can do what you do."

"What, stay here and not fight?"

"Be a normal person."

It was true, normalcy was something that had eluded Yuki since she decided on her unconventional career path in the army. She had little idea of what it would be like to be stuck in one place long enough to actually gain responsibilities for maintaining her role there.

"We're all good at different things," said the woman, fastening the last parts of her elegant orange and yellow garment into place.

"I guess you're right," said Yuki. "Maybe one of these days I'll be a good monster."

"If last night was any indication," her visitor grinned, "you are."

"Wait..." Yuki laughed, slightly taken aback. "What's that supposed to mean?"

"That you... Sorry, that was phrased badly."

"That I devoured you?" she asked, raising one eyebrow.

"I think... I'm not even usually into other women, I just..."

A mischievous smile grew across Yuki's face.

"I get it," she playfully mocked. "Special occasion, right?"

The woman looked down, visibly embarrassed but still seemingly on to the good nature of Yuki's prodding.

"Thanks for the great time," she said, turning back to her.

"Consider it a gift from the gods," said Yuki.

The mysterious woman flashed Yuki one last smile before stepping through the swinging bead curtain and out of her life.

"Hey, I..." she started to say after her, quickly realizing that she was out of earshot. "Never got your name."

But maybe it's better that way, she thought, sliding out of the bed and onto the wood floor.

Her clothes, the temple night robes, still lay on the floor at the bottom of the bed where she had thrown them. Picking them up, she stepped into her shorts and pulled the grey top over her. They were strikingly clean, a benefit of the henshin – none of the dirt from her disembarkation in front of the Maharaja had been present when she materialized.

Reaching into the pocket, her fingers closed around the now-familiar shape of Narajin's gold amulet.

Yuki, his voice boomed through her still-hungover brain. *Good morning.*

Morning, she mentally mumbled before she slid the stone into its notch on the surface and felt her body disappear.

Did I miss anything? Narajin asked.

Oh, not much you would've enjoyed, she said, not entirely sure what exactly it was that he would enjoy at all.

Just as well. The majesty of this place has been continually scintillating along my journey.

Our journey, you mean.

With your return, it most definitely is.

The jungle canopy spread out before her, winding up and around the sides of mountains and across rivers that flowed along their southward trajectory. Whatever lay ahead, it definitely was a sight to take in now. More importantly, the henshin had cured her hangover.

It was a mere hour before they breached the heart of the jungle – climbing to the top of a small cliff with a waterfall embedded in its surface, the trees parted, and facing them was a large clearing. At the center, dominating the landscape, was the magnificent Grand Temple of Ganejin.

A marvelously ornate tower, adorned in statues and carvings depicting the elephant god and his many exploits as a vanquisher of evil in ancient times, it towered a hundred and twenty meters over the canopy, the height of the kaiju himself. Fortunately, they could see that news had reached the temple in time for it to be completely evacuated in the eventuality that Ganejin awoke in a foul mood – not one person remained in the entire clearing, and by assumption, the building itself.

So, Yuki thought as she surveyed the temple, *where do we find him?*

Narajin directed their gaze to a small shrine a little less than a kilometer from the main temple. Covered by a white stone roof held up by four columns, it housed a gold, human-sized statue of the four-armed elephant god that faced the temple with a look of stern authority. Yuki had heard stories about the temple that said the statue had existed for countless millennia, dating far back into ancient times before the recorded history of Avarta had begun.

Like many of the other kaiju, Narajin had told her, Ganejin was born in the bomb blasts that ended the old world – but within each of them was an incarnation of a force that stretched back to before humanity ever existed. Perhaps some element of that force existed within humans as well. Maybe that was the "mana" that Narajin wouldn't shut up about, and maybe that was how whoever built the statue had predicted the visage of Ganejin long before he existed in flesh and blood.

The legends that Yuki heard as a child told stories of how he had gained his reputation as a remover of obstacles, and an impenetrable blockade for any enemy that dared challenge him. He had protected the land of Avarta from invasion and pierced the stronghold of the enemy kaiju in the great war at the formation of the five nations.

A few meters in front of the shrine, they knelt to the ground as Narajin sniffed for the scent of where his brother lay.

He is here, said the monster.

Right here? Alright, are we ready to do this?

We must be.

Having determined that it was the right spot, they lifted their right claw and dug it into the ground. The earth and rocks moved away with relative ease as they excavated, digging straight down with both claws toward the sleeping giant's resting chamber. Large chunks of debris large enough to crush houses flew in every direction as they descended, the hole turning into a cavernous pit twenty meters deep. At last they hit solid stone.

This is it, said Narajin. *The roof of the chamber. We must hurry if we are to –*

His thought was interrupted as the surface cracked and exploded, an enormous hand bursting through the stone slab beneath them and locking its fingers around Narajin's right arm. A jolt of fear ran through them both as they felt the vice-like grip. Ganejin had arrived.

Chapter 8:
Thunder of Ganejin

Yuki and Narajin found themselves airborne. The massive arm protruding from the ground had flipped them head over heels, sending them crashing face-first into and flattening a sizable area of the jungle. Quickly regaining composure, they rose to their feet to see an enormous, four-armed humanoid beast with the head of an elephant staring back at them, a wild and terrifying rage burning in his eyes.

The newly awakened kaiju stood a full twenty meters taller than Narajin, distinctly humanoid, but with enormously oversized musculature – bulky and powerful, with four equally huge arms that ended in disproportionately gigantic fists that looked like they could crush anything they wrapped their fingers around. He let out a sound that shook the jungle, a blood-curdling combination of a trumpet and a roar.

You didn't tell me your brother was almost twice as big as you, said Yuki, her panic almost drowned out by pure adrenaline.

Are you ready, Yuki? Narajin seemed to ignore her concern and went straight for galvanizing for battle.

Yeah. Let's kick some elephant ass!

With a mighty roar, they ran forward toward the enraged beast, claws extended. Yuki could feel the surge of energy as they leapt into the air and dug their nails into Ganejin's chest.

Shrieking in pain, the monster grabbed Narajin with all four arms and tore them away, lifting the great lion above his head and throwing them down as hard as he could. Trees lining the clearing collapsed from the shockwave as every part of Yuki ached from impacting the ground with such force.

Cracking dislodged joints back into place, Yuki and Narajin slowly lifted themselves off the ground and stood to once again face their opponent. They lifted an arm to wipe blood off of their face before extending their claws again and taking a crouching fighting stance, their left arm extended forward and the right raised back behind their head. Completely in sync, their minds whirred together as they strategized.

Is that all you've got, you giant bastard? Yuki taunted confidently, despite knowing that Ganejin couldn't hear her.

Watch what you call my brother, said Narajin disapprovingly.

Sorry.

Ganejin extended his arms out to the sides and clenched his fists. A thunderclap sounded and a flash of lightning emerged from his body as he roared. Yuki was a bit taken aback by the display, but remained focused. She let out a roar herself as they jumped forward with a back kick to the elephant's face, knocking him backwards a few steps. Narajin landed in perfect formation facing away from their opponent just moments before Ganejin grabbed their shoulders from behind and sent jolts of electricity running through their body.

Patches of Narajin's fur began to catch fire as Yuki felt the intense shocks surge down their spine. Determined to end the elemental assault, they grabbed the elephant's arms and somersaulted forward, lifting and flipping him over, smashing him head-first into the ground. The monster's grip released upon impact and Narajin leapt away, stamping out the flames with their paws.

Ganejin stood up and, looking even more enraged than before, turned and stomped over to the main temple. Putting his hands up against the side of the tower, he began pushing it off of its foundations. Yuki remembered the promise they had made to the Maharajah, and realized that the chances of keeping it at this point were pretty slim.

The tower's foundations crumbled as it fell sideways onto the ground. With visible strain, Ganejin picked up the toppled edifice, held it over his head, and began walking toward his brother.

Oh crap, Yuki panicked, *what is he gonna do?*

She already knew the answer. They put their arms up to block the incoming impact just as Ganejin smashed the building over their head. Debris flew in every direction as the stone temple was demolished against the lion god's body, shattering the immense piece of architecture and nearly rendering Yuki and her companion unconscious.

She shook herself awake just in time to see a stump-like foot descending toward their face. It hit, accompanied by the worst pain she had ever felt, again and again as the elephant god stomped on his fallen adversary. With all the strength they could muster, they put their claws out in front of them, caught the foot on its way down and pushed backwards, making Ganejin lose his balance and fall onto his back, letting out a dismayed trumpet.

Pulling themselves to their feet once more, Yuki and Narajin took their fighting stance, ready for whatever Ganejin was going to throw at them next. The area had been almost entirely leveled, the shrine being the only structure left fully intact. The temple had been torn to shreds when the tower fell, and the part of it that remained was crumbling. Even knowing that casualties had been avoided by the prior evacuation, it was a little disheartening to see a thousand-year-old architectural masterpiece turned into a battering weapon and utterly obliterated.

Thinking fast to come up with some kind of way to use what little surrounded them to their advantage, Yuki's eyes transfixed on the fallen trees that lined the clearing. Narajin quickly caught on as they bounded over and picked up a tall tree with a fairly wide canopy that had been uprooted in one of the shockwaves that had shaken the ground. Holding it fast, they sprinted over to where Ganejin still lay, apparently confused by his loss of balance.

Open wide, Yuki sneered.

With their left paw they grabbed Ganejin's trunk and held it to the side as they stuffed the tree into his mouth with the other. The huge elephant began to thrash about in crazed confusion as his brother continued to force-feed him greenery.

So, how exactly are we supposed to get him to calm down? Yuki asked, sensing Narajin's lack of a concrete idea for how to end the confrontation.

I suppose we should have thought this through a bit more, he conceded, the tree disappearing into Ganejin's mouth as the elephant monster chewed the trunk into pulp before spitting it back in their face.

Now you say that! So we just keep fighting him until one of us kills the other, right? Great plan!

With a mighty push of all four arms, Ganejin sent his brother barreling backwards once again and crashing into the dirt. Looking up, Yuki diverted her attention in the direction of what remained of the temple just in time to see a small speck that looked like a person dash out of the jungle and towards the ruins.

Hey, she asked, *is their gemstone amulet connect-y thing in there?*

I believe it would be in the temple – but they do not have a suitable host.

Well it looks like someone's about to volunteer.

She felt Narajin's focus shift and the acknowledgment that he knew what she was talking about. If they were ever going to subdue Ganejin, they would need to connect him to a human host, and hopefully that host would arrive soon.

We have to make sure that person gets to it, she ordered. *Can you hold your brother on your own for a minute?*

The weight of his decision hung heavy in their minds, both knowing full well what the outcome might be.

I will do what I can, he said.

Spit me out towards the temple. I'll catch up with whoever that lunatic is, and we'll see if we can get him to fuse up with the big guy.

Very well, Yuki. Good luck.

A flash of light and a swirling return to the physical sensation of her human body told her that she had separated. The lifting feeling in her stomach and bird's eye view told her that she was being catapulted through the air in the direction of the temple, just as she had requested. Realizing that the ground was quickly rushing up to meet her, she took a rolling position and made sure to land feet first. Her right foot snapped upon contact, but the roll forward kept the impact from doing any further damage.

The pain in her foot was excruciating, but not enough to keep her immobile. Putting her weight on her left leg, she lifted off the ground while scanning the area for the person she had spotted before, catching the shape of a small figure just seconds before it disappeared into a hole that had been broken in the side of the crumbling temple. Shutting the pain out of her mind, she began limping across the field towards the opening about three hundred meters away.

She glanced over her shoulder to see Ganejin throttling his brother with his lower set of arms while bashing against the sides of his skull with his two upper limbs. Narajin looked like he was barely holding onto consciousness as the pummeling went on. If he died, the world would be without one of its protectors, and Yuki's place in the coming fight would be taken away as suddenly as it had come to her - but none of that mattered as much as the prospect of losing perhaps her only friend.

Grabbing the stone hanging around her neck, she instantly felt the concussive, mind-numbing pain that Narajin felt. His was slipping away, but her presence seemed to jolt him awake.

Yuki, he muttered wearily, *I will handle this. Do not burden yourself with my fight.*

It's my fight too! If you go, then what am I supposed to do, asshole?

Very well. But at the moment, I can feel your wounds just as vividly as you can feel mine. We must focus on our own roles in this battle if we are to prevail.

Oh... She instantly regretted her intrusion. *Just hang in there. I'm almost to the temple.*

I will fight as long as you need. But hurry!

Good kitty.

I am not —

His retort was cut off as she let go of the stone. He wouldn't let her down now, and she couldn't let him down either. Crossing the threshold into the temple, it took her a moment for her eyes to adjust to the shadows. The only light coming in was from the hole in the demolished wall, but she could make out the shape of a corridor on the other side of the room. The sound of running footsteps echoed through the ornately carved walls, getting fainter by the second as the mysterious individual receded deeper and deeper into the temple.

Onward Yuki dragged herself, past carvings of Ganejin and the occasional face of Narajin lining the building's insides. Distant booms and a tremors in the floor kept a constant reminder of the battle raging outside, while the faint footsteps before her gave direction through the labyrinthine halls.

Suddenly, the footsteps stopped. A crushing feeling began to wash over her as she considered having lost the person she had been chasing. Just then, a soft light illuminated a doorway a few meters in front of her. The scene reminded her of the passageway beneath Narajin's temple when she had discovered the Priestess performing the ceremony to awaken him. With any luck, whoever this was could join with the kaiju the way she had.

Entering the room, she was greeted by a small, wiry figure slightly shorter than her and much thinner. The person was wearing a dirty shirt and ripped pants, with hair barely longer than a centimeter. Yuki cleared her throat to get their attention, causing them to spin around to face her. To her surprise, she found herself face to face with a skinny pre-teenage boy with a gaunt face and eyes wide with shock and wonder.

"Uh..." she struggled to find the right way to address him, "I'm Yuki. I'm from Narai."

"You're the avatar of Narajin?" he asked in a mature, matter of fact tone not at all befitting his young age.

"Yeah..." Yuki responded, slightly taken aback, "what's your name?"

"Manvi. I've come here to –"

"Yeah, so Manny... we're gonna need you to... but... you're a kid."

"I'm more ready than anyone else to become the avatar of Ganejin. None of the volunteers have yet arrived and if we continue waiting –"

"There are people who are supposed to help with this? Why didn't we know? We would've just waited!"

"Too late now. The temple is collapsing, and when the altar is buried, there will be no stopping him."

"I guess... Great, so you know the whole deal with the turning into a monster thing? We don't have a lot of time, so if we could just..."

A tremendous crash reverberated through the walls from outside as the floor shook and pieces of stone decorations fell and shattered. A million thoughts raced through Yuki's mind regarding what had happened, but remembered what Narajin had told her about focusing on her role alone. Manvi ran over to a crumbled altar and began rummaging through fallen shards of rock.

"Do you know how the amulet works?" she asked frantically.

"Yes, I'm not a child!"

"I don't know, how old are you?"

"Ten. But I may as well be a man!"

"Okay, fine, let's just find this thing."

"I have it!"

He held up a large, green amulet, similar to hers, but covered in blue jewels and made out of solid green jade. In his other hand he held a stone, also like hers, but in the shape of an elephant tusk.

"Ganejin gets cooler accessories," she commented, mostly to herself.

"I'll see you in battle," Manny said as he placed the two together.

Blue lightning enveloped him as he levitated just off the ground before disappearing in a blinding flash. Yuki was impressed, but a little miffed that a kid was showing her up by being seemingly more prepared for this than she had been. Grabbing the stone and her own amulet, she placed the two of them together.

Hope you're still alive, she thought, *I'm coming in.*

Her vision adjusted and a skull-splitting pain washed over her. She had fused with Narajin, who was apparently still conscious. They were lying on their back in the middle of a crater. Ganejin sat cross-legged a few hundred meters away. It looked like he was meditating, and was probably having some sense talked into him by that kid she had just met.

I was gone for like ten minutes!

I am glad to see you too, Yuki.

Narajin sounded exhausted by the ordeal, but seemed to be in good spirits.

Who is Ganejin's human host? he inquired.

Some ten year old kid. Manny. He's like, a genius, or something.

Oh? That is surprising!

He almost seemed to be laughing, exasperated as he was. It was, strangely enough, the best mood Yuki had seen him in despite having just been beaten nearly to death.

So, she asked, *how are you feeling?*

Physically? I could be better. But I am glad to have my brother back with us.

Yuki looked over at Ganejin, still sitting with his back straight, motionless, eyes closed, two hands on his knees and the other two outstretched in a meditation pose.

Hope he's not gonna lose his shit like that again.

Ganejin is communing with his host. When they have fully merged their minds, we will speak with them about the journey that lies ahead.

I take it we're not staying here for long, then.

No. Mokwa and Alkonoth can sense that Ganejin is awake. The enemy will not dare attack Avarta now... Their strategic target now lies in South Pacific, on the islands of Tarakona. If we are to beat them there, we must beat them at their own game.

Yuki worried about what that implied, and knew she probably wouldn't like it.

We're not jumping into any volcanos, she said. *Are we?*

Chapter 9:
Journey through Inferno

Tired as they were, there was something about being on the road again that put Yuki's mind at ease. They weren't fighting an impossible battle, and they now had an impossibly strong ally. Now that Ganejin wasn't mindlessly trying to kill them, she could appreciate his majesty – strutting across the landscape with the confident gate of a master warrior, he looked like a moving mountain capable of lifting a continent. If anything inspired confidence in what was to come, it was knowing that his waking crankiness had subsided and that he was now irrevocably loyal to his brother.

According to Narajin, Ganejin had sworn to protect him and Yuki at all costs. Her companion would have to do the communicating with the other kaiju, which had both positive and detracting side affects. The only voice besides Narajin with whom she had to talk was Manny, who had informed her of the ability for hosts to communicate through an obnoxious intrusion into her headspace. He hadn't attempted talking again after she told him off, even though she was sure he meant well – he was just a kid, and seemed excited beyond bounds at having become a kaiju. How could he be blamed? It was practically a dream come true for someone who had probably spent most of his life pretending it, and was now living it.

So, Manny. Or Manvi.

It's alright, you can call me that.

Cool. You weren't actually a priest or anything, were you?

No. I was too young.

So... Why did...

Why did I almost get myself killed to do this?

Yeah, that.

My family. My father and mother work in the nearest city while my grandmother takes care of us. My brother is in the guard, off at the border in case the Scythians attack. We don't have a lot at home. Sometimes we go to the temple and pray to Ganejin to remove the things that prevent my family from being together. I realized he wouldn't wake up unless I woke him up and joined with him myself.

Yuki's attitude toward the boy was beginning to turn from annoyance to sympathy. He was just a child, but he had gone through hardship that she hadn't experienced in her formative years – she had grown up in a fairly well-to-do environment, and her mother had always been around to support her. She had found herself in dire situations since, and had felt the weight of the world turning against her in its own way, but it was still a vastly different perspective.

My favorite stories, he continued, *are the legends of the kaiju that my grandmother told to me. The story of how Ganejin pierced the evil monsters' stronghold, and how Jhalaragon caught the last of the destroyers before it could escape and together the Pantheon Colossi ended the time of darkness. I hoped maybe one day I could be like a kaiju. Now that I am, I'll make sure my family can have the life they deserve.*

Manny's story made her think about how much she missed her own family, and those she had befriended along the way – even the Priestess, whom she had known for just a few days, but had shown her understanding in her bleakest time. Yuki thought that perhaps that was what brought them all together.

I'm really excited, Manny continued, *because this will be my first time leaving Avarta.*

Giving it some thought, Yuki realized that the journey had been a similar experience for her too.

It's funny, she said. *I hadn't left Narai until... what was that, a week ago?*

How did you like Avarta? Manny asked.

Well... she snorted. *Fight was a little intense, but... beautiful place. Wonderful people. Met a girl, had fun.*

What did you do?

Uh...

Yuki took a deep breath.

Where we're going, she continued, *you're gonna see things. Stuff that'll damage you.*

I'm ready.

You're not. But you know what's not gonna damage you?

What?

Knowing that two women had a nice, romantic night together.

Romance is weird, said Manny, sounding slightly uncomfortable. *But I'm glad you met another nice lady.*

Yuki burst out laughing.

Glad you think I'm a nice lady. Thanks, kid. And don't worry, you've got plenty of time to figure yourself out.

The horizon began to show the jungle's end at the eastern shore of Avarta. From there, it would be a few hundred kilometers of swimming before they arrived at the uninhabited Barren Island, home to an active volcano that would serve as the gateway to their journey through the Earth's mantle.

Sure this volcano thing's not... dangerous? She asked Narajin.

Only for the humans and other animals who live near our entry and exit points. Fortunately, we will be traveling between a desolate, volcanic island and a deep sea fissure off the coast of Tarakona. The enemy will probably not be nearly as careful, and may cause severe casualties at their point of arrival.

If that was the case, she knew they had to focus on stopping the enemy from causing further damage once they emerged. Judging by how well containing a kaiju had gone the day before, she hoped they would fare better with numbers on their side.

Jhalaragon is in Tarakona... Is that gonna be another situation like your brother?

I do not know what stage of finding a host he has reached. He is awake, but beyond that... He is a free spirit, one who does what he likes.

So you don't know?

No. I am not omniscient, Yuki.

As the two kaiju stepped over the threshold of the sandy beach and waded into the ocean, the cold waves of the Avartan Ocean lapping against their body as they rolled in from the bright blue horizon, Yuki felt a lump growing in the pit of her stomach. Even if traveling through the Earth's mantle was safe and expedient by kaiju standards, diving into molten lava and descending miles beneath the surface was still a frightening prospect – but given everything that had happened so far, she wasn't about to stop trying new things.

Choppy, white-tinged surf washed over them as they swam toward the island. The sun's golden rays passed overhead and behind as morning turned to afternoon, and the shape of a smoking mountain appeared as a dot on the water. As it grew closer and clearer, Yuki could make out details – no visible plant life, just solid volcanic rock sloping up to an open caldera.

Orange and purple illumination of dusk settled in, flowing from behind and bathing the island in peaceful hues, if not for the fiery red light emitting from the smoking summit. Their feet hit bottom as they began to rise out of the water and advance onto the shore, Narajin roaring and shaking the water out of his fur.

With silent resignation, Yuki looked up at the mountain they would have to climb. The slope began gradually, before sharply inclining to an almost ninety-degree angle toward the pinnacle. Ganejin was the first to start the ascent, stomping up the mountain and digging all four of his hands into the side of the rock face. Narajin didn't have the advantage of two extra limbs, but they made up for it by using their claws to anchor themselves as they climbed, hooking onto the jagged outcroppings in the rocks.

With one final heave, Yuki and Narajin pulled themselves to the tip of the caldera to see Ganejin standing at the edge of a chasm that fell away to reveal a pit of bubbling, smoking lava several hundred meters below the sharp drop off. They stepped closer to the edge, knocking some rocks into the pit that were instantly incinerated upon contact.

How the hell are we gonna survive that? she thought.

We are impervious to – Narajin began to respond.

Yeah I know, the mana. You've gotta understand how scary this is for a human, though, right?

I suppose I should consider your perspective.

Thanks.

Before they could be the first ones to jump, Ganejin flexed his calves and leapt over the side, turning mid-jump so that he faced head-first, flattening his arms to the sides to form the most streamlined possible shape. The enormous gargantuan kaiju dipped gracefully beneath the surface, only causing a minor splash of lava against the sides of the basin.

See, Yuki, Narajin said, half taunting her, *just like that!*

In one movement, they crouched, pulled their arms in to their sides, and pushed their feet off the edge towards the middle of the basin. It felt like minutes as they fell towards the lava, their heart racing and Yuki's adrenaline pumping. At last the boiling, searing surface collided with their face. First came a burning sensation, but then their sense of temperature evened out and she could feel it – the energy of the molten rock flowing into them.

Opening their eyes, Yuki saw a world of bright red liquid exuding pure energy. What on the surface had looked terrifying now looked beautiful as they descended through the flowing, ever-shifting kaleidoscope of red ribbons and shapes. They seemed to be speeding up as they descended, the lava flowing around them faster and faster as more of its energy seeped through them. At last they stopped descending and made a sharp turn to the side, shooting them through a constant explosion of orange and yellow.

We have breached the crust, Narajin shouted to her, *and are now following a current through the mantle that will take us to the Tarakona Trench.*

What's this feeling? Yuki asked. *It's incredible!*

Pure energy. We are swimming through the lifesblood of the Earth!

It was the most exhilarating, rejuvenating sensation Yuki had ever felt as the full blast of the planet's energy flowed around and through them. The injuries she had sustained over the past several days, both mental and physical, were now gone and in their place was a sense of near-invincibility. The power of life itself seemed to be rebuilding them anew. All sense of relative time and space disappeared as their journey went on. The only thing that they felt was the mesmerizing flow of the lava and the sensation of being alive.

In the short time she had existed, Yuki had seen enough death that it had made her almost totally desensitized to it – but as she flew through the vibrant lava ocean and felt Mana in its purest form, she understood what a powerful responsibility she had been given. It was not meant to be used to take life, but to preserve it. That's what the kaiju were for, in a somewhat roundabout way. If life on Earth was being threatened, the kaiju would fight to protect it from any threat, at any cost.

As with all good things, the euphoria eventually met a rudely abrupt end as the two kaiju were spat out of the volcanic fissure and onto the cold blackness of the ocean floor. The change in temperature was the most extreme Yuki had ever felt, but rather than something to complain about, she felt refreshed by the frigid water after her nine-thousand kilometer Mana swim. Tiny tube worms and deep sea crustaceans moved about their feet as they exited the opening, moving into the dark depths of the sea.

How did you like that, Yuki! Manny exclaimed, clearly having enjoyed the ride just as much as she had.

It was... she struggled to find concrete words. *I can't even describe it.*

We must move quickly to reach the surface, Narajin commanded. *The deep ocean is not a place for kaiju to linger. One never knows when they are not alone.*

As far as Yuki knew, deep sea leviathans hadn't been seen in over a millennium, but Narajin probably knew what he was talking about. Even if they were around, she was sure the two kaiju could take them.

Do not get overconfident, Yuki. We are powerful right now, but we are not invincible. This is not our prime environment, and we must conserve our energy for the confrontation to come.

Fair enough, she said.

Pushing with their legs, they lifted off from the ocean floor and swam upwards, their arms displacing massive amounts of water to propel them from the crushing depths. Ganejin had the benefit of four arms to swim with, but his massive weight kept him at roughly the same speed at which they were traveling. The pitch blackness remained all-encompassing even as they continued to ascend. Yuki thought she caught a glimpse of something enormous moving in the dark just out of reach, but decided that it might have just been her imagination playing tricks on her.

Finally a tiny glimmer of light pierced the darkness above them like a pin prick. It grew as they ascended, bringing dawn to the waters of the deep and giving them a destination. Little by little, pitch dark turned to glittering blue. Yuki took in the image of Ganejin ascending toward the light, a sight more celestial than intimidating. Too bad, she thought, that most people did't see them this way and only saw them when they need to become violent.

Waves gently rolled off their heads as they reached the surface. The sun was shining from the east, signaling that it was mid-morning. They could see both of the Big Islands of Tarakona in the distance, only a few hours swim from where they were.

It was now technically late winter in the southern hemisphere, an interesting change for Yuki who had never been outside Narai, let alone south of the equator. Strange birds flew over, some landing on Ganejin's head without him noticing. The sea was calm, the sun warmed the water, and the scent of the lush environment of the islands filled the air.

As they neared the shore, Yuki could make out small shapes moving toward them. At first she thought they were birds skimming the water, but then she saw that they were made of wood. They were outrigger canoes, but with one pontoon on either side and a huge frill-like sail encompassing the main canoe to catch the wind and propel them forward at blinding speed.

What are those? she asked.

The people of Tarakona incorporate Jhalaragon's image into their technology, Narajin explained.

The enormous lizard's neck frill that propelled him faster than any other kaiju had been replicated to build their boats that traveled from one island to another, across the vast expanse of the ocean nation that stretched from the equator to their current location, deep in the southern hemisphere. Such advanced technology was the only way for a nation comprised of islands hundreds of kilometers apart to hold itself together.

As the boats approached, she could see that there were men and women in them, standing up and waving to the arriving kaiju. Yuki let out a roar to greet them back. Some of them fell over in astonishment at the loud noise, but they remained happy to see the two monsters.

These people don't deserve what's coming for them, she thought.

No one does, Narajin said, his tone severe. *We must do everything we can.*

Tarakona was a paradise in the south seas. The two Big Islands were further south than most of the others, but still near enough to the equator to have a temperate climate in the winter. The more tropical islands were seen as more desirable by some, but the beauty of the Big Islands was unequaled anywhere else in the world, with mountain ranges, grasslands, and canyons carved into volcanic stone.

Tarakona people had thrived amongst the waterways of the Pacific for thousands of years. Their art was famously beautiful, featuring expressive and ornate wood carvings. As they approached the shoreline, Yuki could see an intermittent line of majestic stone statues of stylized humans and kaiju, some stretching tens of meters high.

Torches were lit on the beach and crowds gathered as they made landfall. So far, Narai had given them the coldest reception, while the Avartan government had treated the coming of Narajin with skepticism. Tarakona was the first place that seemed to openly accept the kaiju with such a warm welcome, perhaps from Jhalaragon's active presence in their culture.

As the water rolled off of Narajin's fur and the pads of their feet touched the hot sand of the beach, Yuki couldn't feel more guilty. She knew, at the back of her mind, that no matter how hard they fought to protect these people, there would no doubt be casualties and shattered lives when Alkonoth and Mokwa arrived.

Maybe we should get out and say hi, Yuki suggested. *Ready, Manny?*

I am! he responded cheerfully.

Suddenly, a deep rumble sounded on the far side of the city. A large mountain stood several kilometers beyond the limits, and the sight of faint wisps of smoke began to emerge from its peak as small avalanches rolled down the side and sent a piercing fear into Yuki's heart.

No time, she said.

The mountain, said Manny. *Does that mean what I think it does?*

Yeah. They're almost here.

Turning inward, she focused on speaking to Narajin.

Any word on Jhalaragon?

None. Jhalaragon will have to find us if he is going to join the fight. Otherwise, it will fall on us alone.

Well that's great. Hey, Yuki broadcast to both Manny and Narajin, *maybe if we get to the other side of the city before the eruption, we can at least shield some of it from the blast.*

Yeah, Manny responded, *that's worth a try.*

Narajin silently acknowledged as well, and Ganejin seemed to respond with a small trumpet. It was a last-ditch attempt to serve as some kind of barrier between the people and the coming disaster, but it was the only idea they had. Slowly, they stepped over the panicking crowd and began moving between low-built houses on their way toward the volcano. People moved out of the way and ran toward the beach to take cover. Buildings slowly emptied, the population relocating to shelters on the far side of the city. Even if the volcano had remained dormant, the city was prepared – what they might not be prepared for was what came after. The kaiju stepped over the far boundaries of the city and faced the volcano just as another deep rumble sounded from the mountain, this one louder than before.

Is it starting? Manny asked, sounding for the first time like a scared child out of his element.

Yeah. Hold on, Yuki assured him, *we can take them.*

As much as she wanted to believe that, she wasn't so sure. The odds of the battle would be two against two, but she had seen what the two enemy kaiju were capable of. The last time she had seen them, they had laid waste to the Narai army. Images of the battlefield came flooding back through her mind once again. Immediately, fear turned to adrenaline, and a need to stop carnage like that from happening again.

With the city behind them and the smoking volcano before them, Yuki stood at the ready, waiting for the showdown.

Chapter 10:
Big Rumble in the South Seas

A guttural sound filled the air accompanied by a strong vibration underfoot. The chaos in the city quieted for a moment. Yuki, Manny, and the two kaiju stood at the foot of its slope, gazing upward at the sleeping giant beginning to announce its return.

For Yuki, the wait seemed as interminable as the one before her first battle. She wished the mountain would just blow its top off and get it over with – the rush of oncoming devastation had to be less terrifying than the anticipation.

Another vibration came, this time louder. Some rocks toward the peak dislodged and rolled down the slope toward them. A third vibration soon after shook loose large boulders and sent them raining down on the kaiju. Two of them struck Narajin in the face, but Yuki hardly noticed. The smoke emerging from the peak was thicker than ever, and rocks were shaking free at a near-constant rate.

A fourth vibration began, but this time continued to build in intensity. Narajin's eardrums pounded with the thundering bass sound coming from the mountain.

This is it, he told Yuki. *They are here.*

Inhaling sharply, she braced herself.

Showtime.

For a fraction of a second, a wall of sound crashed into their ears. The summit of the mountain exploded from the top own, ripping itself apart in a titanic supernova of rock and earth. Then silence. Blinding light and a cloud of debris obscured most of what was happening. The shockwave ran over them as they dug their feet into the ground to keep from toppling over.

Through the smoke, Yuki could see fire – molten rock freeing itself from imprisonment as an angry dark cloud ascended toward the stratosphere. The top half of the mountain had been utterly destroyed, the newly minted caldera now bubbling and bursting with a lake of lava. The sun was totally eclipsed by the ash cloud, and burning embers began to rain down.

Lava spewed skyward once more, and an immense shape emerged from the pit. Yuki's heart stopped. Molten rock fell away and flames parted to reveal the familiar silhouette a gigantic bear, a mountain in and of itself, rearing its head back and letting loose a bellowing war cry. Behind it, another shape arose, long and slender, before extending its enormous wingspan to either side and letting out a screech of its own. The image burned itself into Yuki's mind – the burning mountain, atop which the winged, airborne Alkonoth and the hulking Mokwa formed one bat-like silhouette against the flames.

What have they done to you, my friends? Narajin thought aloud.

Still enshrouded in flaming embers, Mokwa slowly turned her head, fixing her mad gaze on the two kaiju standing at the bottom of the mountain. Yuki could feel the bear's eyes burning into her, eyes of a demonic predator that had found its prey. Mokwa let out another bellow and pulled herself from the caldera onto the mountainside. Leveraging hundreds of thousands of tons of pure muscle, she began bounding down the mountain toward them, gaining momentum with every landing. Alkonoth flapped her wings, bringing the gust of a typhoon, and swooped down from the summit, gliding on the volcanic ash-filled wind toward her enemies below. Ganejin moved forward, arms flexed in a fighting stance, ready to meet their challengers

2,000 meters.

1,000.

500.

Just as the enemy kaiju were almost upon them, a sonic boom sounded and Yuki spotted another enormous shape moving faster than anything she had ever seen on land. This one was long and slender, like Alkonoth, but colored green with long, bounding legs on either side propelling it forward at blinding speed, a massive sail around its neck carrying it forward with the howling wind. It screeched as it retracted its frill and leapt into the air. The reptile landed directly on Alkonoth's back, sinking its teeth and claws into the bird's neck.

Jhalaragon! Narajin exclaimed, *always late, but far too swift to miss the battle.*

Mokwa, having gained the momentum of a plummeting asteroid, continued on her trajectory. Ganejin stomped his right foot into the ground as hard as he could, both to challenge her and to anchor himself against the oncoming living tsunami. At last, a thunderclap resounded through the valley as the unstoppable force met the immovable object.

Alkonoth and Jhalaragon rolled onto the ground, the huge ibis poking and stabbing with her beak, at which the mammoth lizard slashed with his razor claws. The avian kaiju tried to flap her wings and escape, but the newcomer extended his sail-like frill encircling his neck, catching the wind coming off of the bird's wings and creating a maelstrom that threw them both backwards and onto the ground. With Alkonoth temporarily down, Yuki and Narajin took the opportunity to launch forward and engage.

Remember me, asshole? Yuki screamed.

They wrung their fingers around Alkonoth's neck with their left hand and prepared slash with the other. Yuki's fury and resentment from their last meeting was ready to unleash on the great bird as she extended their claws and prepared to gouge into its face. Jhalaragon circled, while thunderous cracks sounded from a kilometer away where Mokwa and Ganejin grappled with all their strength in an attempt to topple one another.

Before Narajin could deliver the strike, a sharp talon dug into their leg, sending excruciating pain through their body. Having lost focus for less than a second, they found themselves falling over backwards as the great bird grabbed them with her legs and lifted off the ground.

Yuki looked down to see the battlefield shrink away from them. Ganejin and Mokwa continued their sumo match as Jhalaragon ran to join them. The city lay in ruins from the blast of the volcano. Up the side of the mountain they flew until they were directly over the still-erupting caldera.

Neither had to say a thing – they knew it was the opportune moment to strike.

They lifted their dangling torso up toward their captor, claws extended, and slashed at the bird's underbelly. Alkonoth let out an exclamation of anguish as they slipped out of her grip. Airborne, Yuki rolled into a spinning hook kick and slammed the back of their left leg into the bird, sending it careening downwards. Together, the two monsters plummeted toward the boiling lava pit.

The lava splashed around them, filling Yuki's lungs as they submerged in the sea of bright orange and red. She could feel its energy surging through every vein, every pore. Her mind was clear, her fear disintegrated.

Harness it, Yuki! Narajin shouted. *Use it to our advantage!*

She could feel the lava begin to swirl around her, as if it were obeying her by force of will.

Alkonoth is controlled by a human, but we work in tandem, he said. *The power of two beings fighting together will always be stronger than the power of one!*

Yuki saw Alkonoth moving toward her through the molten lake. Staring into her eyes, she drew their right arm back and brought their left knee in to their torso.

With her newfound command over the elements, she spun around and rocketed forward, extending their right leg into a kick that landed on the top of Alkonoth's head. The momentum of the lava kept them catapulting forward until the two kaiju burst out the side of the volcano and into the open air in a geyser of fire and rock. Bright neon lava flew outward, Yuki and Narajin riding the wave into the crisp night sky, their outstretched right leg propelling their adversary away with them.

Landing on the side of the volcano amidst the glowing molten rock flow, Alkonoth extended her wings to fly away. Before she could lift off, Yuki drew their arm back and directed the volcanic flood against her. The lava hit the kaiju, weighing her down long enough for Yuki and Narajin to reach her. They grabbed Alkonoth by the legs with both hands and tossed them over their shoulder onto the ground. Over and over they lifted the giant bird and smacked them back down against the rocks. Finally, the monster stopped moving, apparently weakened.

Wait, said Narajin, *we cannot kill her.*

What are you talking about? Yuki said, perplexed at the suggestion.

We have to see if we can turn her back from human control.

Reluctantly, she abided and stopped. As they leaned in to see if the monster was still breathing, the bird's eyes opened. In one motion, she reared her head back and pierced her beak into Narajin's chest like an enormous sword. Yuki shrieked in pain as the stabbing weapon crunched through their vertebrae and slashed their internal organs. Their arms shot forward and clutched the bird's slender beak in an attempt to pull it out, but to no avail. At last, they felt the giant weapon change direction as Alkonoth retracted her head. Yuki and Narajin stumbled backwards, glowing green blood pouring from the wound.

I told you we... she began.

Yuki couldn't finish her sentence before they toppled over, their back splashing into the magma. Alkonoth stood up and screeched in amusement at their victory. Tauntingly, she stepped over and skewered her adversary again in the arm, then in the stomach. Finally, she moved her beak up to their face and held it over their left eye.

Just as she was about to deliver the killing blow, a thundering, rolling mountain of monsters impacted Alkonoth and knocked her sideways. Mokwa and Ganejin were locked together in a vice-like wrestling match, throwing themselves in any direction trying to smash the other in a single cacophonous formation. Jhalaragon, seemingly enjoying being along for the ride, jumped on and then off of Mokwa, circling and then jumping on again in an effort to help his ally.

Seeing that Alkonoth was down, Jhalaragon took the opportunity to leap onto the giant ibis and sink his fangs into her neck once again. Alkonoth attempted to scream, but her windpipe was blocked by the attacking reptile's strangulation. He clawed at Jhalaragon's body with his talons, but the lizard would not release.

As the four kaiju engaged each other, Yuki and Narajin lay still in the hardening river of magma, gaping wounds wide open. They stared up at the ash-clouded sky that still rained embers down on the city and the ocean beyond.

Are we dying? Yuki asked.

Not yet, Narajin replied, though his tone wasn't convincing.

I can't feel the mana anymore, she said.

It still exists within you. Search for it.

She didn't know what he meant, but realized that they didn't have much of a chance if she didn't figure it out soon. Closing their eyes, she began to look through her mind, revisiting memories, sensations, emotions from times long past. She thought of her mother, her memories of her father, the Priestess...

Nope, that's not it, she thought.

At least it had reminded her of some nice memories before her life fizzled out.

Wait, is that really what's gonna happen?

It will if you let it, said Narajin

If I let it? Is that really an option? 'Cause if I have anything to say about it, I can't die yet, and you can't either. We've still got stuff to do.

Yes. So how do you plan on living?

Uh... Power of friendship? Isn't that how this stuff usually works?

Remember your elemental control in the volcano.

But we're not in the volcano anymore. From here, that would take... I don't know, all the energy we have.

Then use it all. It is the difference between life and death.

Okay... Okay.

Yuki collected all of her concentration toward finding the focus she had felt when surrounded by the lava. It was much harder from outside, especially in her weakened state, but she could feel her thoughts beginning to take her into the caldera... She could feel the molten rock, sense its fluid movement. She tried to make it move, but couldn't quite forget that she was far away, lying on her back, dying.

Clear your mind, Yuki. Try again.

She closed her eyes and concentrated, blocking all thoughts of physical pain. She felt the Earth moving underneath her, its blood flowing to the surface.

Just bleed a little more for me, she thought.

The caldera began to bubble more violently, the hole they had opened in the side of the mountain letting more and more molten rock emerge. Soon the slow ooze of magma had become a crashing lava river, flowing out onto the mountainside toward them. The four kaiju stopped their battle for a moment to witness the strange event. Harder and faster the lava flowed until it became a torrential flood. It swept across the battlefield, enveloping all five kaiju and sending them floating toward the ocean on a wave of fluorescent red.

Good thing the city's on the other side, Yuki thought as they road the wave coastward.

The lava flow spilled over the side of the land and into the sea, sending the five kaiju plunging into the cold waves of the Pacific. Enormous clouds of steam arose from the water as the lava cooled into magma. Yuki felt her consciousness fade as she realized she had used up the last of her energy to cause the eruption.

Well... It's been a wild ride, she thought to Narajin.

Everything faded to black.

You are not dead, Yuki, he said scornfully. *Wake up!*

A jolt of power ran through her. She realized that the energy they had absorbed from the lava flow had finished healing their wounds and was now giving them the strength needed to continue fighting.

Oh, well in that case...

Yuki and Narajin burst from the water and onto the still-hot, newly resurfaced land. Jhalaragon was the first to join them, looking at them playfully with his forked tongue hanging out.

He seems to be enjoying this a little too much, Yuki thought.

Jhalaragon is a free spirit, said Narajin admiringly, *and I can only imagine that his human companion is as well.*

A third burst of water sounded behind them and Alkonoth emerged, squawking with rage.

On the other hand, Yuki said, *that one is not going to enjoy this.*

Alkonoth focused her eyes on Narajin and charged, beak forward. Yuki took a deep breath and brought all of their newly attained energy into focus. They roared, threw their head back, and let loose a burst of explosive flame from their mouth. The luminous green fireball hit Alkonoth in the face, sending her keeling backwards before toppling onto the cooling volcanic rock, unconscious.

Holy shit!

Yes, Yuki. Through your determination, you have trained your mind to –

We can do that? Why the hell didn't you tell me we could do that?

We could not before. You have found the power within us. You trained your connection with the mana to –

So what else can we do now? Fly? Laser eyes?

No, but through vigilance and training, we may one day gain other abilities not yet known.

Damn... Still cool, though. That was cool, right?

I do not –

Come on, you know it's cool!

Alright, yes.

The surface of the water burst once more, and out rose Mokwa, bellowing with raging insanity.

Oh, shit, Yuki panicked. *We have to do it again! How do we do it again?*

She closed her eyes and tried to summon the energy needed to replicate the attack. Jhalaragon ran at Mokwa, but was easily swatted to the side with one jab of her shoulder. Yuki felt the fire rising inside her. They opened their mouth and expelled another fireball, but Mokwa was ready with an attack of her own – the bear deity unhinged her jaws and out poured a stream of green light that collided with the fireball, causing it to explode in mid-air. The ray continued and hit Narajin in the chest, knocking them over backwards.

Though they were physically incapacitated, Yuki felt Narajin's will to defeat Mokwa through another means – to wrest her from the enemy's control. She looked into the eyes of the monstrous bear, trying to make some kind of connection and see through to what was inside her. Though she couldn't talk to other kaiju telepathically, she could feel something in Mokwa's presence beyond just a giant, mindless creature.

She could almost reach whatever it was - not quite tangible but strong enough that she could feel it emanating from the kaiju's mind. It wasn't a word or a message, but an image – the shore of a lake looking out on two small islands. Something about that place was important enough in Mokwa's consciousness that it was the only part of her Yuki could see.

A final burst of water sounded as Ganejin emerged from the ocean. He charged at Mokwa from behind, grabbing and electrocuting her with all four of his hands. She turned and bit down on his lower right forearm, causing him to shriek in agony and let go. With one final gesture, she blasted him backwards with her ray, sending him crashing into the dirt. She turned and headed back toward the sea, throwing a disdainful look at Alkonoth's unconscious body on her way out. The giant bear disappeared into the waves until only her head and front claws were above water, swimming away to the east.

Yuki began to regain her composure and surveyed the beach, which was now covered in hardening volcanic rock and four incapacitated kaiju. The battle appeared to be over, and as far as she was immediately concerned, the enemy had been stopped. There would be no invasion of Narai from the south, and Tarakona would not become a staging ground for the enemy.

You still there? she asked Narajin.

Yes. He sounded just as exhausted as she felt.

Sitting up, she turned to face the volcano. About a third of it remained standing, the rest of it having been blown to smithereens during the fight, much of the destruction happening of Yuki's own accord. On the other side of the mountain lay the city, reeling from the impact of the initial eruption, but spared from most of what had happened afterward.

The monsters had never reached the populated area, and all things considered, the damage had been kept to a minimum. Still, it pained her to see the smoke rising from the buildings that had been hit by the blast, thinking about all the lives that had been destroyed and loved ones that had been ripped away by a senseless act of war.

Truly a horrible party, Narajin intoned solemnly.

Shocked, Yuki almost reprimanded him for the tone-deaf nature of his joke until she remembered that she had equated the word "party" with an explosion in her explanation to him. Deciding that she didn't feel like correcting him now, she went along with it.

You're not wrong, she said.

Turning her attention away from the disaster, she looked at the three other kaiju sprawled out on the beach to make sure they were still alive. Ganejin lay on his back at the water's edge, while Jhalaragon appeared to be waking up having survived being slammed against a large rock off to the left. Between them was Alkonoth, face down and feathers singed where Narajin had blasted her. Yuki noticed a small, white speck on the ground underneath her right wing. Focusing in on it, she saw that it was a man, lying face down in Scythian uniform pants and a tight, white t-shirt. His head was covered in short, blonde hair and he had an imposingly muscular build. Despite being dwarfed by the kaiju, he seemed to be taller and larger than the average human.

The question of where he came from hung in her mind for only a second before she put it together – he was Alkonoth's host. He was her controller. Slowly, the man's ribcage expanded as he inhaled and his arm moved to lift himself. He was alive.

I'm getting out, she told Narajin. *There's someone I want to talk to.*

Chapter 11:
A Shift in the Wind

Ivan Breshkov was the prodigy of the Scythian legions. The deadliest officer in the army's elite corps, he had been secretly hand-picked by the Tsar himself to "pilot" the kaiju Alkonoth. He was a ravenous animal, inhumanly strong, the perfect killing machine. At least, that was what he told Yuki as she stood pinning him to the ground with one foot pressed down on his throat.

"Of course you are, you piece of shit!" she roared sarcastically at her captive. "Tell me where the next point of attack is."

Unable to find a threat suitable enough to yell at him, she lifted her right foot and kicked him a few more times in the face before stomping back down on his throat. Normally she would have felt some level of remorse for brutalizing an injured man, but this wasn't just a man. In her eyes, he was more a monster than the kaiju themselves, a murderer who had taken the lives her comrades. Plus, he didn't seem to be too concerned about the beating as he spat blood through his permanent scowl.

"You won't get information from me," he growled. "As my family lives and breathes."

Grabbing the amulet hanging on his chest, he withdrew an egg-shaped stone from his right pocket. Before he could put the two together, Yuki stomped on his hand with her left foot, causing him to emit a high-pitched yowl. Standing with her full weight on his wrist she bent down and picked up the stone.

"Give it back!" he barked.

Ignoring him, she inspected the stone, which seemed to be made of the same type of rock as hers, except for a circular piece of metal that had been bored into the side. It had no markings, and was shiny and perfectly flat, like the side of a blade. She ran her finger over it, smudging the surface. Grabbing her amulet, she contacted Narajin.

Are you seeing this? she asked. It took a few seconds for him to respond.

Yes. Remove that metal plate immediately.

She began picking at the plate, trying to pry it out of the stone.

What is it?

Our connection goes two ways, said Narajin. *I can project my mind into you, and you into me. That plate blocks Alkonoth's mind. It causes her to lose free will so that man can control her when they join. I am guessing that is how they are controlling Mokwa as well.*

Wait, it's that easy to take control of your minds?

That is why we must trust the people with whom we join. Alkonoth clearly trusted him. She was wrong.

She looked down at the gagging, scowling man beneath her and thought about all the carnage that had been caused by Alkonoth in this bloody war.

"It was all you," she muttered, mostly to herself.

"And I'd do it again," he spat.

Ignoring his last remark, she put her fingers underneath the metal plate and pulled as hard as she could. With great strain, it ripped out and sent dust flying into her face. She coughed a few times, then handed the stone back to Ivan.

Alkonoth will now have a say in their control, right? she asked Narajin.

He will.

"Ok, Ivan," she sneered, "if you use that thing again, you're going straight into Alkonoth's mind, except this time it's a two-way street and we both know she's gonna be pissed. If you want an angry kaiju who probably wants nothing more than to smash you into the ground sharing your head with you, then go ahead and knock yourself out."

Ivan looked at her in painful frustration. His scowl clenched and his eyebrows rose as he realized there was nothing he could do to get himself out of this situation.

Just then, the wing of the downed kaiju that sprawled out next to them lifted slowly into the air, particles of debris falling onto them. The body of the beast rumbled as the creature awoke, her head looking up from the ground and surveying the area. Her surprised gaze went from one kaiju to the next, letting out a squawk when she saw Narajin. Cold fear began to creep up Yuki's spine as she remembered what a confused, groggy kaiju was capable of doing.

Alkonoth's eyes slowly drifted from Narajin to the ground just beneath him where they landed on Yuki and Ivan. Her eyelids widened and her face quivered as rage appeared to build. Ivan clutched Yuki's leg as he stared death in the face. The great bird shrieked and lunged forward, her blade-like beak stabbing at the ground. Ivan and Yuki rolled to the side, narrowly dodging it. Again the beast's towering muzzle rose and then plummeted toward the ground, and the two humans swerved to avoid being impaled.

To Yuki's surprise, Ivan showed no fear – clasping the stone, he stared Alkonoth in the eyes with a look of resignation, as if he understood exactly why the beast lashed out and was prepared to receive her retribution.

Deciding that the quarrel was between the man and the monster, Yuki grabbed her own amulet and fused back into Narajin.

Oh, wow, she thought, *it's much more entertaining from up here.*

From above, she could see Alkonoth's fierce staring contest with the tiny human sitting on the ground in front of her.

It is not entertaining to me, said Narajin. *Alkonoth is dealing with betrayal, pain, and horror at having realized her complacence in the deaths of humans.*

Looking at it that way did indeed make it less entertaining, but there was still something satisfying about watching the stare down. At once, the giant bird stopped and sat down, a defeated look overwhelming the fury that had engulfed her.

Wait, she's not gonna kill Ivan? Yuki asked, disappointed.

Revenge will not make things right, Yuki.

Wonderful, time for another lesson in morality from the giant cat.

I am not... There is something you must understand. Alkonoth needs a human host if she is to continue with us on our journey.

Our journey? Yuki asked, puzzled by the statement. *To where?*

That is what we must find out from Ivan, and Ivan is the only person who can fuse with Alkonoth at this time. That is why we he must live.

Wait, so we're bringing him along?

He will not harm Alkonoth again. We will make sure of that.

Yuki hated the idea of associating with this man she perceived as a war criminal, but it appeared they had no choice. At least he would have to answer to their demands now. By this time, Ganejin and Jhalaragon were waking up to the bizarre scene.

Hey, Yuki, are you there?

Hey Manny. Yeah, and we've got a new addition to the family.

Who is... Oh, that guy?

It's a long story. He's a murderer named Ivan, and he knows things that we need to know. Why don't you meet me down there and we'll talk to him? Maybe kick him around a little more?

Sounds like fun.

The two of them disembarked and materialized on either side of the Scythian prisoner, still within breathing distance of the sulking bird kaiju.

"Hey, guys!"

The voice sounded from behind them. Turning around, Yuki saw a tall, dark tan-skinned man in grey calf-length shorts, sandals, and an open black denim vest approaching them across the freshly hardened basalt.

"Who are you?" Manny was the first to address him.

"Yata! So great to meet you in person. What a crazy day, right?"

"Yeah..." Yuki said apprehensively. "Look, we'd love to meet fans, but there's some stuff we need to take care of first."

"Right on, lemme join in then!" he said throwing his hands out to the side, his tone almost as relaxed as his loose body language. "Unless I'm kicked off the team right after I saved your asses like that."

"What..." Yuki stumbled, "you're Jhalaragon's host?"

"Oh, whoops!" he said, putting the back of his hand over his mouth in embarrassment, barely hiding his friendly smile. "Yeah, that's me."

"Well, this is an interesting development," grumbled Ivan.

"I didn't say you could talk!" Yuki shouted down at him.

The Scythian snorted and looked down at the ground in frustration. Yuki turned back to their new acquaintance.

"So what's your name? I'm guessing you're Narajin's host, right?"

"Yuki," she said nonplussed. "This guy down here is Ivan, and if you can tell from his appearance, he's from Scythia."

"Right on," he nodded, his enthusiasm scaling back slightly without quite losing his positive demeanor.

"I'm Manvi from Avarta," Manny interjected, seemingly excited to have a new friend. "Yuki started calling me Manny for some reason, but I kind of like it."

"Manny!" Yata said, his smile practically beaming off of his face. "Good to meet you my dude!"

"What's the deal with not showing up until the last minute?" Yuki asked. "You scared the shit out of us, and that kinda pisses me off."

"Honestly?" said Yata, his relaxed tone becoming slightly more defensive. "We didn't know what side of the volcano the monsters would come out of. We were watching for volcanic activity since way before you guys showed up – Jhalaragon knew something was up when he sensed that other monsters started waking up and going on the attack. It was honestly lucky that you got here in time. Otherwise, we would've had to take them on ourselves."

"And what makes you think you could've done that?" said Yuki.

"Nothing. We would've died."

His honesty and humbleness was appreciated – what she had perceived as arrogance at first was just, as Narajin had said, a free spirit.

"Well, you're welcome," she said.

"It was my pleasure to fight alongside you guys," Yata said, his smile returning. "Look at us... just some cool people who turn into cool monsters."

Yuki half wanted to roll her eyes and half wanted to give him a high five, but couldn't find it within herself do either. Still, she couldn't stop herself from smiling, much as she visibly tried to fight it. His enthusiasm was absolutely infectious, and he seemed to at least be an enjoyable person to be around. Moreover, he completely fit Narajin's description of Jhalaragon, which amused her to no end. She wondered momentarily if she was somehow similar to Narajin in the same way, before snapping back to more urgent matters.

"As for you," she snarled, turning toward Ivan and forcing an angry expression while trying to sound as menacing as possible, "we still need information."

Ivan looked up at her, clearly a defeated shell of himself despite the facade of fiery stubbornness he still wore. At last he closed his eyes, breathed deeply, and gave in.

"You had friends in the Narai army," he said softly.

This statement infuriated her more than anything else.

"Yeah," she spat. "Yeah, I did. I was in that battle as a foot soldier. Do you know what it's like fighting a kaiju as a foot soldier?"

"No," he said, refusing to raise his voice in return. "It is not something I will go back on, as I did it for my own reasons. I did it for those that I care about. For your experiences, and your losses... I am sorry."

It was the very last thing she had expected him to say, and it certainly didn't make her want to forgive him. It did, however, make her think twice about her attitude toward him as an adversary. She had, after all, killed humans by her own hand in a regretful exertion of power.

"Alright, I know you're not gonna forgive me," said Ivan. "I don't need for you to see me as a good guy. Just... hear me out. Maybe we can work together."

"And why would I want to work with you?" she asked.

"Because if I'm right, then something really bad is about to happen."

"About to happen? As if what's been happening isn't bad?"

"Like I said, just hear me out. The Scythian legions will not continue the campaign without Alkonoth on their side. The Empire does not have the strength or the will to continue the war on our own, and our alliance with the Laurentians was based on a deal. They would send Mokwa to help the Tsar gain control of Narai and show us how to control Alkonoth. Once Narai was taken, I would return with Mokwa to Laurentia and help carry out their part of the plan."

"Their part of the plan?" Yuki felt a lump forming in her throat. "What about the invasion?"

"Without the kaiju, Scythia can no longer advance into Narai." he continued. "Not that it would've been able to hold it anyway. The Empire is collapsing into turmoil – the war has taken everything. The Tsar will not be able to maintain power much longer."

"But what about Laurentia?" Yuki demanded. "Aren't they going to invade?"

"Our alliance was always built on unstable ground. We would have dominion in the East, but we would always answer to them. They have something big planned, something in which they wanted Alkonoth to partake."

"What was it? Tell me!"

"I heard rumblings. Alkonoth was to carry some kind of weapon – an artifact of the old world that they found in the mountains of Laurentia. They spent years trying to unlock its power. They said that if they could replicate it, it would mean the return of humanity's dominion over the Earth. Their leader called it... the return of the great civilization."

Standing up slowly, Yuki tried to take in what she was hearing. An artifact of the old world, granting near-infinite power. It sounded frighteningly familiar.

"Atom fire," she whispered.

"What?" Manny asked.

"That's..." Yata interjected, "there's no way they would do that. They'd be marching us to extinction."

"I'm sorry," said Manny, "what are you talking about?"

"The war that ended the old world." Yuki muttered, terrified. "If I'm right, they found a weapon that can do it again."

She turned back to Ivan.

"You just went along with this, knowing what could happen?"

"I never wanted it. I had to choose between watching my family starve and taking part in a war I didn't believe in, and I'd make the same choice again."

Ivan looked down and wiped his hand over his face.

"I..." he began, softly. "If we get there..."

Suddenly, he looked up and around at his captors.

"There are four of us," he said. "Four daikaiju. That's almost the whole Pantheon. If there is a chance of stopping them, we are it."

As much as it pained Yuki to find herself agreeing with anything this man said, she knew he was right. She looked up and faced each of her companions - Manny, still bright-eyed and ready for adventure; Yata, standing with a determined expression on his face, far more serious than before; Alkonoth, who had experienced so much pain, but still had the fire of a battle-ready kaiju in her eyes. Ganejin and Jhalaragon stepped closer to the circle of warriors, ready to partake in their ancient duty to protect the planet. Yuki turned around to face the last warrior present, putting her hand around the amulet that brought their minds together.

I am ready, Yuki, Narajin said. *If a few humans have chosen to decide the fate of all, then we must do everything in our power to stop them. We must go - to Laurentia, to Mokwa, to unite the Pantheon Colossi!*

With the last statement, he let out a blaring roar. The other kaiju joined him, trumpeting and shrieking triumphantly. The other humans seemed to get the gist that it was a call to battle, as Manny and Yata both raised their fists in the air and whooped enthusiastically. Even Ivan found it in himself to smile.

"Looks like we're all in," said Yuki.

Manny and Yata disappeared in flashes of light and smoke while Ivan looked worriedly at his amulet.

"Don't even think of trying anything," Yuki snarled, "not that she'll let you."

Refusing to look at her, he zapped into thin air, joining with the giant ibis who would undoubtably give him mental hell for everything he'd done. Yuki grabbed her own amulet, and in an instant, she was back with Narajin, looking out at the sea across which they would have to travel.

Oh yeah, she thought to her companion, *how exactly are we planning on getting to the other side of the world? Another volcano?*

No, we must be less conspicuous. Luckily, we have Alkonoth and Jhalaragon to help us with that.

Just as he had spoken, Alkonoth and Ivan extended their massive wingspan and lifted off into the air. Jhalaragon unfurled his frill and sprinted into the water. Ganejin grabbed onto the reptile's shoulders as the sail caught the wind, and together they sped off into the Pacific, sending ocean spray rocketing into the air on either side of them. Yuki was barely able to grasp what she was seeing when two great talons grabbed onto Narajin's shoulders and lifted them skywards.

The ground sped away and they ascended into the clouds. They were flying – not of their own accord, but they would be making the trip to Laurentia by air nonetheless. After everything that had happened, and all the horrors that she expected lay before them, Yuki was amazed that she could still feel complete wonder and joy at another new experience. Beneath them, Jhalaragon sped through the water dragging his elephantine comrade in tow.

It was moments like this when Yuki realized that there might still be hope of overcoming the darkness ahead. Alone, the kaiju were only capable of what their individual abilities allowed. Together, the Pantheon could accomplish wonders.

Chapter 12:
The Mysterious Continent

Clouds flew over, beneath, and around them – faint wisps streaking overhead in the stratosphere while huge vapor islands floated in the atmospheric ocean through which they swam. The bird kaiju pierced the side of a white wall, enveloping them in the cold, dewy condensation. Yuki could feel the droplets landing on Narajin's fur like tiny life-giving water sprites dancing across the mammoth creature.

Alkonoth burst from the other side of the cloud and the sun bathed them in radiance. Night had come and gone in the time they had been flying. Despite being clutched by the shoulders with the talons of a massive bird for all that time, Yuki didn't feel nearly as uncomfortable as she would have expected – or at least, she didn't notice. Seeing the open ocean from above was one of the most liberating things Yuki had experienced – nothing but blue water and blue sky extended as far as she could see, the ocean wind blowing past them. Far below, Ganejin held fast to the back of Jhalaragon as they continued their brisk sea voyage, chopping through the ocean surface and leaving a towering swell in their wake.

The far continent of Laurentia was almost a complete mystery to anyone who lived in Narai. They knew it existed, and that a powerful civilization had managed to build itself out of a land that had been desolated during the apocalypse. Travel by sea was almost impossible due to both the distance, and the inaccessible nature of the continent itself. She had heard stories of Tarakona explorers who had tried to sail west across the Pacific to Laurentia and had never been seen again.

The only nation to have communicated with the Laurentians in centuries was the Scythian Empire, who traveled via a passage in the Arctic Ocean. Yuki considered asking Ivan if he had ever been there, but she decided to avoid the unpleasant experience of speaking to him. Besides, if she was going to hear about this place, she would rather hear it from Narajin, someone she trusted much more implicitly. The trajectory of the kaiju was taking them northeast from the South Seas, which meant they would have to breach the great coastal barrier of Laurentia.

The distant horizon began to darken. Tall clouds rose up like black mountains, specters of an oncoming storm. Beneath them, the blue of the water disappeared into dark, churning waves punctuated by white foam as they smashed against each other.

We are getting closer, Narajin said.

Is that the barrier? Yuki asked.

No. You will know when you see it.

The four kaiju crossed the ominous threshold into the storm. Yuki could feel a little colder, a little less euphoric as they dipped below the clouds and closer to the water so as not to fly blind. Sheets of rain poured down thicker and thicker until Yuki's field of vision was restricted to the torrential downpour thrashing against their face.

Lightning flashed and silhouetted immense, jagged shapes covering the horizon. It was only barely visible for a fraction of a second, but it looked like some kind of hellish mountain range protruding from the ocean.

Manny, Yata, she yelled, *are you guys still down there?*

Yes we are! Manny replied, as chipper as he could sound given the circumstances. *We've hit some bumpy water but it's not terrible.*

That's a huge lie, Yata interjected.

Are you seeing what's up ahead? Yuki asked them.

No, Yata responded apprehensively. *What?*

She could barely think of words to describe what she was seeing. Huge crags of rock jutted out at canted angles from the churning water, each at least a mile in length. It was less a mountain range and more the shredded remains of what was once part of a continent that had long ago sunk into the Pacific, leaving behind only a ravaged corpse of broken Earth.

Oh... Manny gasped, *I see it.*

There was a moment's pause before Yuki sensed panic beginning to set in with the crew down below. The massive shards of rock and collapsed land rendered swimming through the barrier impossible, which meant Jhalaragon and Ganejin would need to find some other route.

We have not time for that, Narajin warned, *we must breach the coast tonight if we are to apprehend the Laurentians in time.*

Yuki looked down at their friends, who were beginning to slow down as the waves grew higher and harder in their pummeling. Ganejin held to his reptilian companion for dear life, both of them looking distraught and confused at what they should do about their predicament. Carrying them over might be too much a strain on Alkonoth, Yuki thought. Other options seemed to evade her as she considered that this might be the end of the line for the Pantheon.

We can carry them, Ivan's voice pierced into her mind.

It took her a moment to get over the unwelcome sound of his voice to realize that this was actually a welcome suggestion.

Uh, are you sure? she asked, *It won't be too much for Alkonoth to hold all of us up?*

It was her idea, he replied, *and if we can't then it will be the same as if we do nothing, right?*

A selfless suggestion coming from the psychopath was the last thing she expected to hear, but it was the best plan anyone had at the moment, and they needed one.

If you guys want to carry us then now would be a good time, Yata shouted to them from below.

Okay, Ivan yelled back, *the big one first.*

Alkonoth slowed their flight and lowered them gradually toward the thunderous waves and the two kaiju afloat amongst them. Ganejin looked up at them as they descended, locking eyes with his brother.

I'm going to grab on to your hands and legs, Manny yelled. *Hands first.*

The elephant kaiju raised both of his top arms toward Narajin, holding fast and inadvertently dunking Jhalaragon underwater with his other two. Yuki and Narajin reached out their arms toward the great beast, almost reaching but being swung away at the last moment as Alkonoth's uneven flight veered off to the side in a gust of the typhoon winds.

Hold steady up there!, Yuki shouted.

You try flying in this, Ivan retorted, clearly struggling.

Again they descended toward the elephant kaiju, arms outstretched and ready to make contact. Swaying left to right, Narajin reached for their brother's fingers, always almost in reach and then slipping away. The waves poured over the two floating monsters, Jhalaragon now completely out of sight as Ganejin stood on his back to stay above surface. Giant waves splashed Narajin in the face. They cleared the water out of their eyes just in time to see Ganejin's hands sticking out of the ocean, as the great god of Avarta sunk into the depths.

Ivan, take us down! Yuki commanded.

Alkonoth dropped like a rock, plunging Narajin into the water just in time to grab Ganejin's arms as they went under. The two brothers locked their hands around each others arms for dear life as the tsunami-sized waves thundered overhead.

Now, lift us up! Yuki shouted as water filled Narajin's mouth.

With a tremendous push of their wings, Alkonoth lifted them slowly out of the water. Ganejin grabbed onto his brother's body with his other set of hands, distributing the weight more evenly and making Narajin feel less like their arms were about to be ripped out of their sockets.

As they ascended, Jhalaragon emerged from the water, the comparatively spindly monster hanging onto Ganejin's legs and gasping for air. The ocean fell off of them as they lifted toward the dark swirling clouds, the storm raging above and below them.

Aha! Ivan laughed.

Hearing him make any kind of positive sound was a bizarre experience, but he had aided in rescuing half of the Pantheon and for that they were all grateful. In that moment, the differences of the past were put aside and the four kaiju lifted skyward. Their collective energy fed them, Alkonoth holding Narajin, Ganejin holding on to his brother with all four arms, and Jhalaragon dangling but holding steady.

They lifted up into the clouds, the jagged shards of continental destruction passing far below them. Yuki wondered what had driven the earth to shatter like it had here, and if the ancient humans had a hand in it. She tried to understand the conundrum of whether the people of the old world knew the devastation they were bringing unto themselves, and whether the Laurentians realized they were on the verge of doing it again. It was not an invading, malevolent force that caused the land to break and the sea and sky to churn into a perpetual storm, but willful ignorance.

As the storm clouds began to separate and the sky lightened, the ground began to grow more solid and less hazardous-looking. The four kaiju were crossing over the barrier and into the western Laurentian desert. A few trees were to be spotted here and there, but mostly there was very little in the way of life. Still, at least the sun was out. The soil was a deep red, and the air was calm. The that looked more like it had eroded away by wind for millions of years than beaten into oblivion by a fractured atom in one afternoon.

They set down on the searing hot ground, crashing into the dirt one after the other in a long row of exhausted monsters. Ultraviolet rays pelted them, recharging their strength and bathing them in searing heat, a welcome reprieve after the journey through the barrier.

Hey Ivan, Yata's voice sounded through the group, *thanks for picking us up back there.*

Don't mention it, the Scythian responded. *Just doing my job.*

I thought your job was to kill for your empire, Yuki snorted.

My job is to protect my friends. Who that is, is all relative to what side you're on.

She hated that yet again she was sympathizing with the man who had killed her captain.

Bad things happen when people go out to kill each other, he continued. *But we're fighting for the same thing now. We're all in the same Pantheon.*

Silence followed, before she broke it again.

You're right. Thanks.

Don't mention it.

This is nice, Yata interjected, clearly trying to change the subject. *Reminds me of the desert continent west of Tarakona.*

You've been there? Manny asked, apparently flabbergasted.

Yeah, with Jhalaragon. Mostly inhabited by nomads wandering around in one big desert. He likes it, there's a lot of space to run around. He was telling me that apparently there's another continent with an entire civilization south of Laurentia and two others to the west of Avarta and Scythia.

Alkebulan, said Yuki, recalling the book she'd read not too long ago.

That's one of them! They don't associate with the five nations for some political reason. I think it's because the kaiju used to... you know.

Yeah, she said. *I can completely understand that.*

I wish I could go there, said Manny.

Let's just get through this first, said Yata.

Chapter 13:
The Burial Mound

The southwestern desert of Laurentia sprawled out from the coast, engulfing all who set foot upon it in a blinding shower of UV rays that poured through a hole that had been blasted through the ozone by ancient pollutants. Lifeforms there had adapted over thousands of years to live in such intolerable conditions. Tiny, blue-green cacti peered out of cracks in the sandy rock ground as small reptiles with a black, tank-like armor of scales scurried in and out of their burrows. The rolling armadillo, once a four-legged creature that scampered underfoot of humans, had lost the use of its arms and legs and had evolved into a limbless armored carapace that curled into a ball of solid bone plating and rolled through the sand, not daring to expose its skin to the deadly light of day and only unfurling itself when it had reached the shelter of an overhanging rock.

Savage and relentless to most lifeforms, the environment of the sun-baked desert was a paradise for a band of kaiju. The unfiltered sunlight gave Yuki a constant stream of energy, endlessly refreshing after the grueling trip over the barrier. Still, they made sure not to needlessly expend themselves, as they would need all the energy they could store when they reached the Laurentian Central Complex on the far side of the desert.

Narajin had explained that they were to be as diplomatic as possible given the circumstances. They were technically at war and were deep in the aggressors' territory, but he hoped that their status as gods would at least allow them an audience to find out just what the Laurentian military program was up to, and hopefully reach some kind of agreement before the line was crossed.

Yuki wasn't entirely sure that the plan would play out accordingly. By all estimations, Mokwa was back within the borders of Laurentia, doubtfully far from the LCC to which they were headed. If she could be called in to deal with them at a moment's notice, the Pantheon's leverage would be minimal at best.

At the same time, Yuki's mind was fixated on the incident in the dead lands, when she had smashed the defenseless battalion of Scythian troops with one stroke of her hand. At least Ivan had the decency to own up to his crimes. Narajin was the only one who knew what she had done, and she wasn't entirely sure how the others would react if they found out. What frightened her the most was that she wasn't sure she wouldn't do it again. Maybe Ivan was right – in a war, every side is a villain to someone.

Hey, uh, guys? Yata interrupted her thoughts, springing her back to reality. *What's that?*

Just now visible through the clouds of dust, a walled structure stood about ten kilometers away. Its drab, steel-plated fortifications rising roughly a hundred and fifty meters high made it look like a large military outpost, a banner hanging over the forward wall sporting the symbol of Laurentia – a single white star on a black background. Behind the walls stood two gigantic, metal chimney-like structures that slanted forward at a forty five degree angle toward where the monsters stood.

Suddenly, the tip of one of the columns let out a momentary burst of flame and smoke. A faint whistling sound filled the air, growing louder as it drew closer. A small meteor-like object crashed into the ground just in front of them accompanied by a cacophonous explosion that blasted Yuki and Narajin off their feet, sending them toppling into the dirt and kicking up an impenetrable dust cloud.

Armor-piercing artillery cannons, Narajin exclaimed as they quickly righted themselves and regained composure. *Their military has recreated more than a few relics of the old wars.*

Well, what do we do? Yuki asked.

We can travel outside the range of their cannons. It is the only way to avoid a fight. However...

Yuki waited for Narajin to finish the sentence, but he remained in contemplation.

But what? she asked.

Then they will send a wireless communique to the Central Complex. They will call in Mokwa to meet us there for battle, ruining any chance we have of –

Alright, so what do we do?

Once more, there was silence on Narajin's end. Another shell whistled toward them, this time striking Ganejin square in the chest, the explosion barely causing the elephant monster to flinch, but evoking an annoyed trumpet.

Guys, Yata said worriedly, *do we have a plan?*

My brother wants to attack, said Narajin. *We may have no other choice.*

So we take out their facilities, said Yuki. *Disarm them. Stop them from* –

They have proven a threat with their war machines. Now we must destroy them.

Yuki, she heard Manny's voice interrupt the argument. *Ganejin wants to —*

I know, she said, *I'm getting the same thing over here. Are these guys right here really a threat? They're not gonna kill us with those things. Why are they acting like this?*

I think I know, said Ivan. *Alkonoth fears nothing except what the Laurentians are planning to unleash.*

That's not here, though, said Yata.

Narajin, Yuki turned back to the monster. *Are we really gonna take them out because of this?*

Humans are about to destroy the Earth and finish what was started long ago, he responded, his voice now a low growl. *We have to stop them at all costs.*

Another artillery shell impacted Jhalaragon on his right leg, causing him to lose balance and fall to the ground on his side before climbing back to his feet.

Dammit! said Yata. *We're either gonna attack or we're gonna move. Which is it?*

Silence set in, broken only by the whistle of another fired shell, Yuki and Narajin moving to the side to avoid getting hit and letting it blow up in the sand next to them.

Alright, said Yuki, the weight of the decision hanging on her. *We'll attack. Who knows what they'll do if they send word that we're here – they might even preemptively use their new weapon.*

That's a good point, said Yata. *Are we ready?*

As ready as we'll ever be, said Manny.

Remember, Ivan muttered, *this one is on you.*

Ignoring his statement, Yuki prepared for what was to come.

Ganejin let out a bellowing trumpet and plowed forward. Yuki felt a surge of exhilaration as Narajin roared, dropped to all fours, and followed suit. Alkonoth took flight, grabbing Jhalaragon on their way up. The great bird flew toward the fortress, swooping low as it approached the walls. Clearly unprepared for an areal attack, the cannons began firing at will, all missing their target and sending exploding shells raining down onto the empty desert.

As Alkonoth crossed into the airspace over the wall, they let go of the monstrous reptile, dropping him right on top of the the enemy. Jhalaragon screeched in battle-ready fury as he disappeared in a cloud of debris upon impact, the screams of the people inside filling the air.

In a single bound, Narajin vaulted over the wall. Beside them, Ganejin smashed through the edifice, sending bits of shattered metal flying in all directions and flattening the building in front of him.

Pops of igniting gunpowder filled Yuki's ears as the soldiers fired upon them. Drawing on the boundless energy she had absorbed, they took a deep breath as the flames of rage welled up within them before exhaling. A ball of plasma shot down at the attackers who were instantly incinerated. Buildings were engulfed in the explosion, their inhabitants blown out of windows or flung through walls on fire, some culling the will to run away before succumbing to the flames.

Metal screeched and cracked as Ganejin pushed against the towering cannons. The massive machines toppled and fell, crushing several other buildings below them. Screams could be heard as Alkonoth and Jhalaragon laid waste to two other cannons on the opposite side of the base, the reptile decimating the edifices with swipes of his tail as the ibis flapped her wings, sending a furious hurricane wind down upon the remaining structures and razing what was left to the ground.

The smoke and debris from the chaotic destruction mixed in the air with the dust of the desert, making the details of the battle nearly impossible to see. All that Yuki knew for sure was that there would be no survivors to tell of what had happened here. The monsters continued until there was nothing left to destroy, and all movement on the ground had stopped.

The dust cloud hung over them as the four monsters ceased their rampage, catching their breath and waiting. An eerie silence set in as they stood amidst the ruins now returned to the desert. The air remained stagnant, the wind refusing to blow. A sinking feeling began to swell in the pit of Yuki's stomach as she realized the amount of death that they had visited upon this spot. Slowly, she began to feel as if they had made a terrible mistake.

Just when it began to seem unbearable, a gentle gust of wind began to move the dust out of their field of vision. Gradually, the debris particles cleared from the air and floated away into the desert, carrying with it the smoke of hundreds of fiery deaths. As the ground began to become clearer, a horrified shock pierced through Yuki's heart. Manny let out a whimpering scream and Yata half shouted an expletive under his breath.

There were soldiers, hundreds, burnt and pulverized into bloody stains in the dirt. Yuki had expected that. What she hadn't expected were the civilians. Twice outnumbering the soldiers, the pulped carnal streaks and shards of regular clothing that had once been their bodies adorned a large area of the settlement that was not a military base at all, but a small town that shared the space inside the wall with the army encampment. The outside of the leveled buildings had the trappings of the military, with banners and other markings to indicate that they were barracks, armories, and other strategically important parts of the war machine. The interiors, however, proved to be homes, places where regular people had lived, dressed up to deceive anyone looking at them from the outside.

She felt like she was going to throw up. Narajin must have as well, as together their stomach lurched and a stream of molten lava poured forth from their mouth. Ganejin staggered backwards, realizing too late that he was stepping on the bodies of the innocent, causing him to let out a disgusted shriek and fall over through a remaining part of the wall. Jhalaragon slumped down and hung his head low in grief, while Alkonoth stood motionless, staring at the ground in front of them.

This... Ivan seethed, his voice boiling over in confused anger. *This isn't what I...*

Do you think we wanted this? Yata barked, punctuating the sentence with a frustrated scream.

This was murder. Ivan sounded like he was about to explode. *Never killed civilians before, but here we are. First time for everything. Shit.*

In a fit of frustrated rage, Alkonoth attempted to flap their wings and take off into the air, but couldn't focus enough to stay airborne and crashed head-first into the desert.

Yuki heard a faint sobbing. It took her a moment to realize that it was Manny. Ganejin was still laying in the ruins of the wall, motionless, too emotionally compromised to even stand. As brave and intelligent as he had shown himself to be, she sometimes forgot that Manny was just a child, and she couldn't even imagine what this must be like for a child to go through. She wanted to tell him it was going to be alright, but she couldn't get the words out – nor did she believe them. She couldn't think straight, or even piece together the reality of what was happening.

Forgive me, muttered Narajin.

No, I'm sorry, Yuki responded. *We should've known.*

It is too late for that.

Too late? she snapped. *What does that mean? They knew we were coming. They provoked an attack knowing that it would lead to a slaughter of their own citizens.*

There was silence as the other kaiju turned toward them.

Don't you see what this is? she yelled. *They wanted us to instigate the master stoke in their war, to be the aggressors! Now they have every justification to use their atom fire.*

Well that's great, Yata shouted back, *what the hell are we supposed to do about it?*

Continue the mission.

Continue? Just walk into the Central Complex and... do what, exactly?

Stop them from ending the world, Manny said.

They all turned to Ganejin, who was standing with his back to the ruins, looking east into the desert.

No one else will do it, he continued.

The kaiju of Avarta turned his head slightly toward them, but his eyes remained fixated on the horizon, absent from the moment but contemplative and focused on the path ahead.

Ganejin is too big and too strong for the world he lives in. But he's my friend. You're all my friends, and we've seen things no one should see and done things no one should do, but we still have to keep going. If we stop now, everyone will die anyway, so there's nothing else we can do about it besides finish what we started. There's no choice besides... Just keep going.

As mature as he had always presented himself, this was the first time Yuki had heard something like this come from the boy they had found in Avarta. Perhaps it was because he hadn't yet been diluted by cynicism as most above his age usually were. Most would have said that he was naïve, but at a time like this, maybe it was what they needed.

What they had done was enough to psychologically destroy a person of any conscience. Yuki knew that was what the enemy wanted, to destroy their will to continue. The only way to get past it was to do as Manny said – just keep going. Unless they made peace with this horrifying debacle, the mistakes of the past would withhold them from the future for which they had fought so hard.

As the sun set upon the desert, Ganejin and Narajin dug an enormous grave in the earth while Alkonoth and Jhalaragon gently deposited the bodies. The burial mound resembled a small hill, a naturalistic monument to those whose lives had been taken away. Upon completion, the four monsters slowly circled the hill before standing and facing it on all sides.

These humans are now returned to the Earth, Narajin began solemnly, speaking to his brethren and to Yuki. *Their life essence will become one with the planet's, and the ripples of their lives will continue until the end of the universe. We vowed before, and we will again now – that no more innocent lives shall be extinguished by our hands.*

Ganejin let out a mournful trumpet and Alkonoth coo'd softly.

As much as Yuki tried to think of something to say to feel like the deaths had been for something, she could only think of the tragedy's meaninglessness. All it did was serve as an example of what would happen when the tides of war reached those who were not part of the fight.

No more, Ivan muttered, apparently on the same train of thought. *No more of this.*

The sun descended into the sand and the cold of night washed over them like an icy blanket. The four kaiju turned their backs on the burial mound and headed east, the weight on their shoulders far heavier than it was when the day began. Their next stop was civilization. Yuki feared what they would find when they got there, but she knew there was nothing to do about it.

Just keep going.

Chapter 14:

Houston

The first rays of dawn streaked across the desert from the east, drawing a hulking silhouette. A massive industrial mountain appeared as if a mirage on the distant horizon, a titanic construction that lay a hundred kilometers ahead of the kaiju but reflected the morning light and filled the oncoming vista. A mind-bogglingly huge pyramidal city of gleaming steel, its towers extended kilometers into the sky, increasing in height towards the center where two central pillars ascended past the cloud cover and into the heavens beyond. It appeared almost as if it were a pair of columns holding up the sky. Even its base wall completely dwarfed the kaiju.

There was only one place Yuki had seen this kind of engineering before – the lost city in the dead lands near Narai. Differentiating between them was that this place, Laurentian Central Complex, was not a ruin that had lay abandoned for millennia. Smoke emerged from the tops of its towers as tiny people moved across its areal walkways like mites on a twig. It was very much inhabited, and kept in upmost repair.

Rather than move on from what little was left of the old world as the other nations had done, the Laurentians had rebuilt the ruins and lived in them like the humans of old. What had been a mere fable to Yuki was proud history for the inhabitants of the mysterious continent, and they had spent the last five thousand years striving to regain its legacy of industry and power. A goal, Narajin warned as they drew nearer, that they were dangerously close to achieving.

Despite nearing their destination, the spirits of the Pantheon hung low with the crushing reality of the previous day. Images of the smashed corpses filled Yuki's thoughts, always managing to creep back from the corner of her mind to which she tried to banish them. With every attempt to focus, to stay attentive to the task at hand, they pierced back to the forefront of her attention and sent her heart beating into her throat, threatening to catapult itself out of her in a flood of bloody projectile vomit.

Judging by the coldness of Narajin's presence and the silence of the rest of the human hosts, she could be certain that their current state was not dissimilar to hers. Though they were mentally linked, the four humans had never felt more distant from each other. Manny's innocent quips were no more, and Yata's vibrant, sarcastic commentary was now an icy wall of introspective seclusion. Ivan, who had until recently exuded resentment for his fellow companions, now seemed more defeated and regretful than ever. Yuki wasn't even upset with him anymore, so much as she was upset with herself. If the enemy had aimed to break their spirits before they even arrived, they had been successful.

It's, uh, a little weird that they don't even notice us, Yuki finally broke the silence, the first time any of the Pantheon had spoken to each other that day.

A few seconds passed before anyone took up the invitation to respond.

They notice us, Ivan murmured in a guttural half-whisper, *they're just playing along.*

Out of all the members of the group, Ivan had far and away the most dealings with the Laurentians. It was, after all, the reason they had brought him along. A week ago, Yuki would never have thought she could trust someone like him with anything. Now, if anyone was going to find a way to deal with the isolationist regime of the fortress before them, she knew that he would be one to do it.

The Central Complex's commanding shape swelled and overtook the flat desert until it was all they could see before them. Brown, stained metal walls with gigantic rivets and iron patchwork to mend wounds left by the apocalypse made the kaiju look like tiny children. The wall around the base of the city topped off eight hundred meters in the air, impossibly tall by any standards except for the two soaring towers at the middle of the city.

The Pantheon's journey came to an end at the base of the wall, before a kaiju-sized iron gate. Clearly not part of the city's initial construction, the gate appeared to be latched over a hole that had been torn haphazardly through the wall's surface. Yuki mused that perhaps it was collateral damage left over from the kaiju war – it would have taken strength equal to that of Ganejin to breach the city. Perhaps it had been one of the ancient destroyers that Mokwa had stricken down in the last battle of Laurentia.

This is where you must continue without us, Narajin's voice boomed through Yuki's head.

It certainly wasn't what Yuki had expected to hear at the end of their journey, about to walk into the stronghold of the enemy.

But... she struggled, *You're not coming?*

This battle must be fought with wits, not strength. Our enemy will react with force, and our very arrival within the Complex may be seen as an act of war. We must find out more about their weapon if we are to stop its use.

But what if they... I mean, we're just humans. We're marching right in and it's just... us.

You cannot always rely on our power, Yuki. There are some things you have to accomplish without the aid of physical might.

I don't know anything about politics or negotiating, though!

You know more than you think you do, Yuki. We will still be here beyond the gate, waiting for you. Contact me if you must, but I believe in your ability to do this on your own. You possess great cunning and intuition. Now is the time to use them.

Okay... Okay.

Exhaling slowly, she pulled her mind away from Narajin's. The world flashed before her as her perspective and body changed back to that of a small woman in loose-fitting clothes and hallway slippers standing on the burning desert between four kaiju and the precipice of an impossible fortress.

Three plasma bursts sounded around her as she turned to see her human companions materialize. It was the first time they had all disembarked since they left Tarakona, and none of them looked at all comfortable with finding themselves in their current predicament. Manny's face had gone stone cold in stark contrast to his usual demeanor, while Yata's attempt at stoicism barely hid the fear in his eyes. Ivan looked just as expressionless as usual, but Yuki had gotten better at reading the subtleties. Beyond the battle-hardened seriousness of his face, he was as frightened as they were.

"So," said Yata, still deadpan in an attempt to hide the nervousness in his voice, "I take it they all told you the same thing?"

"It's on us from here," Yuki said. "Hold on to your amulets. If anything happens, we zap back to them. No hesitation."

"If we do that, we'll fail the mission," Manny grunted disapprovingly.

"Yeah, but I don't trust the Laurentian government. Do you?"

Silence hung in the air for a long moment before being broken by Ivan.

"No. I have never trusted them, but we must complete mission. We leave only if we know we have failed. They're stubborn. We offer them something in return, and maybe they'll listen. If they don't accept..."

He let out a short whistle and pointed behind him to the kaiju. They nodded in agreement.

"What do we offer them," Yata asked, "any ideas?"

"There's only one thing they want," replied Ivan.

"Well there's got to be something else they want," Yuki said, exasperated, "can't we offer them resources or something? Trading?"

"Try to tell them that," Ivan retorted incredulously.

"It's all we've got," Yuki replied sternly. "It probably won't work, but it's our only option. We've gotta use it."

A deafening metal screech sounded from the gate in front of them. Immense gears began to lock together and turn, chains rattled, the ground shook. The hundred-meter-tall doors began to swing open slowly, the city opening itself to the travelers like an enormous mouth ready to swallow them whole. Yuki's heart raced, her eyes widened, and she held her breath.

As the doors parted, they revealed a line of guards dressed in padded militaristic uniforms. It wasn't the usual battle armor Yuki was used to seeing in the Narai army, but close-fitting green jumpsuits. In their hands were mechanized weapons with long barrels that she assumed were rifles. The advanced guns appeared refined and deliberately manufactured like everything else about these soldiers, down to the way they held their posture. They were a far cry from the four misfits standing before them, and far more imposing.

Trying to downplay how intimidated she felt, Yuki looked past the troops and saw what appeared to be a dimly-lit city of relatively small two-to-three story buildings that looked ready to crumble at a moment's notice, if they hadn't already. The people who had filed into the garbage-strewn streets were dressed in rags and covered in grease and filth. Their disheveled appearance was in stark contrast with the clean, sculpted look of the military personel.

Without stepping forward, one of the soldiers stomped his boot to the ground as if to draw their attention.

"State your business!" he shouted in a mechanical, matter-of-fact tone, still staring straight ahead and not making eye contact with any of them.

"W-we..." Yuki stammered, taken aback but still trying to present as impressively as possible, "We represent the nations of Narai, Scythia, Avarta, and Tarakona."

"You represent their governments?" the soldier barked.

Yuki paused, thinking the question over. The kaiju were guardians of the five nations, but neither their governments nor their people had any idea what they were doing.

"We... We do not," she responded. "We represent the lands of those nations, the kaiju who founded them. We represent the Earth. We wish to speak to your government so that conflict may be averted –"

"You are not affiliates of the four nations," the soldier interrupted, "you are master-less warriors invading our country."

"This is not an invasion!" Yuki barked back, "We're here on a mission of peace. Please grant us an audience."

"Chief Executive Frank Houston demands your audience."

The relevation both surprised her and made her feel uneasy.

"He wants to meet with us?"

"We will escort you to his council chamber and you will divulge all information that he requests. Is this clear?"

Yuki turned to her companions, who stood stone-faced, in shock at the entire exchange.

"Yes, we understand," she replied, "lead on."

In unison, both ends of the line of soldiers moved forward, closing in around the four travelers in a pincer formation until they had completely surrounded them. Yuki gave her friends a nod as the commanding officer shouted an order, and they filed together into the gate.

As the doors screeched closed behind them, Yuki felt the pit in her stomach grow. This was it – there could be no screwing up and there would be no second chances.

With each step they progressed further into the dark, dismal place. Only a few stray rays of sunlight made it past the towering structures over their heads and illuminated strands of the dust-filled air. Denizens of the city slums scurried to get out of the way of the convoy, staring inquisitively at the newcomers.

As they passed, an old woman locked eyes with Yuki. Her expression was that of desperation, someone who had lived a full life of hardship and had been dealt little good fortune in return. She appeared sickly and malnourished, and there was something about her expression that seemed like her mind was not entirely present. Yuki searched for a glimmer of hope in her eyes, the sign that their arrival could signal a change for the better for these people – but there was no hope to be found. The moment passed, their eye contact broke, and they moved on.

"Who are these people?" Yuki asked, mostly wondering out loud to herself.

"They're the scummers," the soldier nearest her replied under his breath, "they live on the ground level with the nuclear fallout. Hundreds of generations spent frying in the dirt. It used to be worse. Now you can walk through here and come out fine."

"Of course you can," said Yuki, sickened by everything she was hearing. "Fallout doesn't last five thousand years. The only thing wrong with these people is that they're starving."

"Whatever it is, they're fine where they're at. We just let what we don't need trickle down here."

The soldiers continued down the main street, past kilometer after kilometer of dilapidated slums to a cylindrical, iron cage-like structure that extended up into the ceiling high above them. Inside it at the bottom was a smaller cage, just above the height of a human, with a locked gate.

A guard standing outside opened the gate and the party filed inside. It was extremely cramped, but they all managed to fit. Yuki stood right next to Yata, who gave her a look that signaled his uneasiness about the whole situation. The gate clanged shut behind them and with a lurch, they began to ascend upwards with a loud metallic rattle.

Sunlight blasted through the exterior of the cage as they shot through the roof. It took Yuki a few seconds to get used to the brightness before she could see the vertical city flying by them as they continued ascending. Yuki had never been this high off the ground while not in the body of a kaiju, let alone in a metal cage filled with people being pulled upwards by a cable.

She could now see through the buildings and over the wall, revealing a beautiful view of the desert that extended far to the west from whence they had come. The kaiju were nowhere to be seen, probably too close to the wall and obscured from sight. The elevator cage was free-standing, allowing them to see the city on all sides, steel towers riding alongside them as the areal walkways connecting the huge structures came and went with the changes in altitude.

"Has one of these ever fallen?" Yuki shouted to the squad's leader who stood next to her.

"Every once in a while," he replied. "Sometimes the cable snaps. There's a lot of strain at this speed."

"Fabulous."

One by one, the tops of the towers began to fall away as they soared past them. Soon the view was comprised of two skyscrapers on either side of them and the open sky. Their ascent started to slow as they apparently neared their destination kilometers in the air. At last, the elevator lifted itself through the floor of an aerial platform and clanked to a halt. The gate opened, and the soldiers filed out, pushing the four visitors with them.

The platform stretched between the tops of two immensely tall buildings. Afraid of being blown over the edge by the billowing winds, Yuki stayed at the dead center of the platform, but could see well enough that they were above the clouds, and her trouble taking deep breaths indicated that the atmosphere had become thin. The horizon was clearly visible in every direction – desert in most cases, but the distant peaks of mountains cropped up to the north indicating that there were other topographical areas of Laurentia they had not yet seen.

"You will now enter the Chief Executive's office," shouted the officer who had addressed them at the gate. "You will speak only when he allows, and you will not disrespect him in any way, under penalty of death."

The officer motioned for the visitors to follow him toward the south tower. Upon reaching the entrance, he stopped.

"You will continue from here."

"You're not coming in with us?" Yuki asked.

"No, I'm not permitted. The guards inside will deal with you if you do anything regrettable."

"Fancy that," she said as the door opened and the four of them stepped across the threshold.

The office was an enormous, circular, domed room taking up the entire top floor of the tower. On the far side of the shiny marble floor was a large wooden desk at which sat a widely-built, pale man with greying, neatly trimmed hair. Not bothering to look up, he continued signing a stack of papers on his desk and whistling a relaxed-sounding melody with which Yuki was entirely unfamiliar. He was dressed in expensive-looking, intricately tailored clothes – a blood red jacket with a white frilled shirt underneath.

"Come on closer," he said gently, still not looking up from his work, "I'm not gonna eat you. What am I, a monster?"

Aware that it was barely-veiled personal jab, Yuki decided to ignore the last comment and slowly stepped across the marble floor toward him. The others followed suit, stopping just in front of his desk.

At last, the man looked up and smiled, squinting at them before placing a small pair of glasses in front of his eyes.

"There you are... Warriors of the world, come to stop the big bad empire."

The pleasantness of his inflection only served to make her that much more uncomfortable. Still, she thought about what the officer outside had told her and held her tongue.

"You are a funny bunch. A lady, a kid, an island man, and... Hey, I know you!"

He pointed at Ivan, grinning ear to ear.

"You're that prickly Scythian son of a bitch who was driving our big bird! Guess you know your folks back home should expect a visit real soon."

Ivan looked like he was ready to rip the man's head off with his bare hands, but he inhaled sharply and barely kept his composure.

Apparently bemused by the entire situation, the man at the desk sat smiling at Ivan for an extended moment before chuckling softly.

"I'm just kiddin' around!" he exclaimed emphatically, throwing his hands up. "Now..."

He shifted forward and scanned the group slowly before locking eyes with Yuki.

"Business time. Go on, gimme the spiel."

"We're here to make a deal," Yuki said in a commanding tone without breaking eye contact, "for the betterment of all nations."

"Ooh!" Houston vocalized excitedly, rubbing his hands together. "I do love a good deal. So here's how it usually works – you ask me for something, then I say no, then you say 'but wait!' and offer me something I want, but then I don't want it enough to give up the other thing so I throw you in jail and get both. But I'm feelin' good today. I'm gonna listen to ya."

Taking in the gleeful ramblings of the man in front of her, Yuki paused for a moment to collect herself. He clearly had some form of intelligence, if lacking in any and all regard for other humans.

"We guarantee," she continued, "that if you give up your quest for atom fire, the other four nations will open their borders to you. Resources, trade, all will be made available to this hemisphere. You have much to gain from a peaceful alliance. You have nothing to gain from a dead Earth."

The Chief Executive's expression slowly drifted from amusement, to annoyance, and finally landed on smug pity.

"Miss... I'm not gonna gain anything from holding hands with savages. The only way to peace is through superior firepower, the great deterrent. Nobody fights if they know they're gonna lose."

"Sir, if you use the bomb it'll end the world all over again –"

"Lady, don't think I don't know! We've got scummers living in the basement of our great city! Sorry, I know it's incorrect to call them that, but... Why do you think the rest of the world is so damn backwards? No offense, but you don't have cities like this over in your countries, do ya!"

"You scavenged all of this from a civilization that blew itself up," Yata burst out, "and you take credit –"

"Whoa, whoa! The island man is offended! Sorry mister, but Tiki huts ain't Laurentian Central Complex."

Houston paused for a moment while he adjusted himself back in his chair.

"There is another deterrent," he said. "Something I want from you people that would mean I wouldn't have to use the bomb."

His gaze drifted down toward Yuki's chest as he licked his lips. It took her a moment to realize what it was he was looking at, among other things.

"No," she commanded, grabbing her amulet. "Absolutely not."

"Oh come on, they're just animals. They're monsters, they smash things. Under our command, they'd be... Police, just watching over the territories, making sure everything is up to our high standards."

"I have only met one real monster," Ivan interjected menacingly, "and it's you."

"Hey," the Laurentian leader responded as if pulling an idea out of the air, "you don't happen to know anything about a town west of here... A military base with civilian settlement. We haven't received any word from them since yesterday..."

Yuki stood in silence trying to collect herself to speak with a man who was clearly trying to manipulate them into the exact places he wanted them to be. The scariest part was that she wasn't sure whether or not he was succeeding.

"You'll never have the kaiju," she said. "They saved us from the brink of extinction, you can't just –"

"Oh, but we can. And we did. Remember your friend the bear?"

"What you've done to Mokwa is unforgivable," shouted Manny.

"But we did it – and according to my intelligence," he said, pointing in Yuki's direction, "this cute doll's country almost did it too. Frankly, I'm surprised you're not in command of the damn thing yourself, unless... oh!"

Houston began chuckling to himself as he locked eyes with Yuki.

"You're not the one they wanted, are you? You weren't even supposed to be here! Otherwise I'd be talking to someone I could get, but with you... I don't need your approval or forgiveness or to ride on your goddamn high horse. That's why I'm always gonna be ten steps ahead of you. This transaction is over. We have an outcome, and it's my old favorite."

As soon as the last word had left his lips, he put two fingers in his mouth and let out a loud whistle. Eight armed guards emerged from the sides of the room and closed in on the visitors.

"Henshin," Yuki screamed, "now!"

"Oh no, you're not morphin' out of here," Houston sneered as he pulled a small golden revolver out of his desk and pulled the trigger with a loud bang.

Yuki felt a surge of pain in her right arm that caused her to let go of the stone that channeled her link to Narajin. She heard the lion's voice echoing faintly through her head, asking her what was happening. He sounded distraught, panicking. His voice disappeared altogether as her amulet was yanked off of her neck by one of the guards.

"I will kill you!" Ivan's voice echoed through the room repeatedly. "I will kill you!"

As the four warriors were dragged out the door and back onto the platform, she saw Houston lying back in his chair, crossing his feet on top of his desk.

"Both is always my favorite," he yelled loud enough for them to hear. "I just love it when I get both!"

Chapter 15:
Autumn of the Earth

A dance of swirling red and gold was performed through the crisp air. Two parts of a living whole had reached the end of their lives and now tumbled end over end, fluttering around each other in a descending spiral as if to evade separation in their final moments. Life itself would continue without them, but first would come the cold winds and bitter grey of the time between.

Autumn had come to northern Narai. It was a spot Yuki had frequented as a child visiting her grandmother. She had enjoyed walking and looking up at the trees as their colors grew warm in the vivid sunset of the year before winter. Her grandmother had long since passed like so many swirling leaves, but the cycle continued and this time Yuki could see it from above – the tops of the trees stretching for miles and miles, up the sides of hills and mountains in a rolling ocean of comforting hues.

It is beautiful, Narajin commented. *Our world has never looked more alive.*

But isn't winter when everything dies? she asked the lion god.

Yes, Yuki. That is why the time of autumn is when we hold on to life the most.

Together they sat on the hillside, observing the melancholic passage of time and the end of seasons – until Yuki awoke.

The view inside the cell was far less glamorous than that of the dream. She wished she could return to it, but the first rays of dawn drifted through the bars on the tiny window and told her that she wouldn't be sleeping again for a long time. The pain in her arm still throbbed with the bullet inside, but she was mostly able to drown it out by diverting her thoughts elsewhere.

Yata lay sprawled out on the floor a little more than a meter away, still fast asleep, while Manny lay on the cell's one piece of furniture – a rectangular concrete slab – looking up at the ceiling with dried tears in the corners of his eyes. Ivan sat motionless on the floor in the corner, knees pulled in to his chest, staring at the wall in front of him.

The dream reminded Yuki that the seasons were indeed changing. She had completely lost track of the time she had been on her adventure with Narajin and the Pantheon, but the fact that autumn was here meant that her birthday had passed without her so much as noticing. She didn't like celebrating it, and didn't think that getting a year older was something she should be reveling in at this point in her life. Still, it was strange to think that here she was, sitting in a Laurentian prison cell realizing not only that the world was about to end, but that she was now thirty years old.

Her thoughts drifted to what Houston had told her about the Narai military. Was she really the only thing that had stopped them, by complete accident no less? What had happened to Ken Sakurai that barred him from completing his mission? Would she ever have a chance to find out?

Footsteps of heavy boots sounded on the tile floor of the barren hallway outside. A guard walked past the cell, dragging a metal stick across the bars, making a loud clanging sound on each one. Yata jumped off the floor and shrieked, much to the guard's amusement. Wiping his eyes and scowling, he quickly lost his entertainment value and the guard moved on.

Yata exhaled heavily.

"What the hell are we still doing in here..." he grumbled.

"Well we don't really have an escape plan," said Yuki, almost under her breath.

"Too bad we don't have anything to bribe the guards with," he said facetiously, "great negotiators we are. At least Houston has things he can barter with, we've got –"

"Will you shut up? We've lost our link to the kaiju, and we may as well have doomed all of civilization."

"At least we're staying positive!"

"You two," yelled Ivan, not turning his head from his corner, "quiet!"

He appeared to be concentrating intensely on a small speck of dirt on the wall.

"Looking at anything interesting there, Ivan?" Yata prodded.

"They have the amulets," he growled, a mixture of anger and defeat.

"That they do..."

"You realize that this means they will control the kaiju in less than two days."

"Wait, where do you get – oh, right."

"It took us years to figure out how to get a signal blocker onto an amulet. Installing it was two days."

"Then there's still time," said Yata, his spirit picking up, "we just have to..."

"Escape?" Yuki added, unexcited.

"Well if we can call in the kaiju to –"

"We don't have our amulets. They're never going to know where we are. I even lost my stone."

"Actually," Manny interjected meekly as he reached his hand into his pocket, removing it again to reveal an egg-shaped stone that Yuki recognized all too well.

"Manny, you picked it up! You saved it for me!"

"I thought you might need it later," he added, sitting up and placing it in her outstretched hand.

She turned the stone over in her fingers, examining it as if expecting to see some kind of clue to aid in their escape, but all she saw was the same old stone.

"You know, it's pretty much useless without the amulet." she said.

"Not necessarily," said Manny, "we've all developed a connection with the kaiju. Maybe you can still reach them in their thoughts. Clear your mind and –"

"Alright, well if I'm gonna clear my mind I'm gonna need quiet."

Clutching the stone tight in her palm, she closed her eyes. She tried to picture Narajin in her head, before realizing that wouldn't do any good – his mental presence was a different thing altogether. The second thing that came to mind was her dream, where they were joined together sitting on the hill in Narai. That feeling of two beings telepathically communicating with each other was unlike any other. Through her mind she searched, looking for the corner where the residual part of his presence resided. It was a vague, ethereal feeling, but one that she could recognize instantly.

She called out – her voice, the image of the cell, the tower in the Central Complex where they were being held – anything that could reach him and let the kaiju know that they needed their help.

"You! What's that in your hand?"

The harsh voice snapped her back to reality to see the guard peering through the bars at her.

"I'm talking to you! What is it? Give it to me!"

He held out his right hand through the bars, palm up, motioning toward her with his fingers.

"Give it to me or I'll come in there and get it," he sneered menacingly, holding the metal rod in his left hand up over his shoulder.

Just then, a loud explosion sounded from outside and shook the tower, accompanied by muffled screams and the sounds of a great number of firearms being shot off.

"What..." the guard exhaled before losing interest in the cell mates and running off to see what was happening.

Another explosion shook the tower, this one closer. A roar and a trumpet could be heard briefly through the wall.

"Get back, away from the window!" Yuki commanded.

The prisoners flattened themselves against the bars, bracing for what was coming next. The wall exploded and collapsed outward, a cloud of dust and debris momentarily veiling what was going on outside. Through the smoke reached an enormous finger covered in blood-red fur and tipped with a sharp claw. A familiar roar blasted against their ear drums, signaling that rescue had arrived.

"Everyone grab on!" Yuki shouted.

The escapees climbed onto the giant claw and into the palm of the hand to which it was attached. Yuki wrapped her arms around and latched her legs into tufts of fur. With a great lurch forward, they flew out of the cave-like prison and entered the sunlight, giving her a vertigo-inducing view straight down the side of the kilometer-high tower of which Narajin was hanging onto the side with his other arm and legs. The paw lifted, and Yuki felt herself ascending toward Narajin's shoulder where he held his hand, signaling that it was time for them to find a more comfortable perch and give him back the use of his left claw.

As soon as they climbed onto his shoulder and latched on, the great monster lunged into the air, giving them a few moments of terrifying weightlessness before landing on the roof of another, smaller tower closer to the edge of the city. Soldiers swarmed up platforms and walkways chasing the beast, firing after them ineffectively. Some shots grazed patches of fur near Yuki, but none of them found their mark on her.

The sky darkened as a shadow passed overhead accompanied by an avian screech. Yuki held tight as Narajin's body rocketed off the ground, claws of a giant ibis pulling them into the sky. An occasional stray bullet whizzed past, but with every flap of her wings, Alkonoth brought them farther out of range of their attackers.

Yuki reached for the string around her neck to thank Narajin for the relatively smooth rescue, but remembered that her means of direct communication with him was gone. Despite the loss of the amulet, though, she could still sense that he was glad to have them back. The mission might have been a failure, but it was just a setback. They would find the amulets – and there was one of them who might know where they would be.

When the city had dwindled to a vague shape on the southern horizon, Alkonoth lowered her flight closer to the ground. The steadfast figure of Ganejin stood below them, imposing even when being viewed from hundreds of meters overhead. Jhalaragon circled around him, looking up excitedly at the incoming escapees. With about a hundred meters left between Narajin's feet and the ground, the great bird began loosening her grip, only to be hissed at by the lion as if to remind her that he had passengers who would not have appreciated being dropped to the ground while hanging onto the creature's fur. Instead, Alkonoth lowered them gently until Narajin was able to stand on his own accord before letting go and touching down next to them.

Carefully and steadily, Narajin leaned his body forward and held his arm out until it lay flat on the ground. Her muscles aching from the strain of holding on, Yuki exhaled in relief as she let go and slid onto the sand, the three others collapsing next to her. Every muscle in her body ached from the sheer forces of riding on the arm of a hundred-meter-tall monster. All she wanted to do was lie there and pass out, but there were more pressing matters at hand than her own comfort.

"Ivan," she shouted, turning to her left to see him sprawled on the ground in a similar position between her and Manny, "you know where they took them, don't you."

Turning slowly to look at her, he lifted his left eyebrow – a rare sign of expression on his hardened face.

"Not exactly," he said, "but I know where they might. Weapons research facility. North, in mountains. The location is secret."

"You know where to look, though," she prodded, "right?"

"I know the area, but we have to cover lot of ground."

"Well if we split up, we can –"

"We can't communicate over distances."

The reality of not having the ability to do any of the things they had gotten used to as kaiju was beginning to set in.

"The monsters can," Manny interjected, sitting up and joining the discussion. "If one of them finds it, they will let the others know."

"Then let's go with one of them," Yuki asserted. "We'll go with Alkonoth, she can cover the largest area."

Yuki looked up at Narajin, knowing that they would have to go separate ways for the time being if they were ever to rejoin. She realized just how attached she had become to the big cat. The beast's eyes locked with hers, deep emerald green oceans of wisdom that shone starkly against his red fur. It was a rare moment between them outside of each others minds. Being able to think every thought to each other without ever coming face to face somehow seemed lesser than this did now, unable to speak a word. Maybe it was just separation causing her to miss their back-and-forth, something she was surprised to now find natural.

At last, Narajin turned his gaze sharply toward the other kaiju and let out two staccato roars. Ganejin pounded the ground with two of his fists in acknowledgment, while Jhalaragon rustled his frill and jumped to his feet. A powerful gust of wind nearly knocked Yuki off her feet as Alkonoth took flight, only to land next to Narajin and, as delicately as a hundred-meter animal could, moved a single talon in Yuki's direction.

She leapt backwards so as not to be crushed in case the giant bird had a minor slip. The dust kicked up and swirled around Alkonoth's claw, which lay outstretched and beckoning for them to climb aboard.

"I guess we're going," Yata conceded as he stepped toward the giant claw, "back on the old kaiju express. Gonna be a great day for my shoulders and elbows."

A violent lurch upwards and they were off, hanging onto the middle talon of the great ibis thousands of meters above the ground. Below them, the other three kaiju split off running toward the mountains – Ganejin angled to the west, Jhalaragon to the east, and Narajin straight to the north.

Desert passed from under them and became rocky foothills, showing faint signs of plant life. It seemed that the further they got from LCC, the less Laurentia resembled a wasteland. Rather, as Yuki looked out to the north, she could see above some of the peaks to a vast sea of deep orange and gold, reminiscent of the autumnal colors of Narai. It didn't appear to have been baked in ultraviolet rays like the desert, or festering in industrial grime like the ground level of the city. It looked pristine, as if the natural world had bounced back over the past five thousand years. Through their desire to wear the skin of the dead civilization they had inherited, the Laurentians had sealed themselves off from the beauty that lay just beyond their reach.

As they sailed over the first mountaintop, the freezing air began to solidify in Yuki's lungs. She tried to cough out the icy condensation, but her breaths still grew continuously shorter and the feeling in her hands continued to fade.

Just when she was afraid her body would begin shutting down, Alkonoth jerked to the right and swooped down between two high mountain peaks, spurring Yuki to hold on with all of her strength. When she had a chance to look up, she saw a small plateau in the midst of the mountains. On it was a wide, single-story building that appeared to be built into a short cliff face. There was no sign of life, but there was no way of knowing who or what was inside.

As Alkonoth landed on a rocky crag opposite the plateau, Yuki looked across to see Ganejin's head peeking out from behind a similar protrusion on the other side. It must have been him who called Alkonoth to this place. The creature's elephantine face surveyed the scene for a minute longer before snorting and rising out of his hiding place, huge hands pulling his body weight up the side of the cliff face.

"What is he doing?" Manny whispered frantically behind Yuki. "He should wait for the others to get here."

Yuki understood the frustration of not being able to communicate with the monsters, especially in this instance when Manny could very well talk some sense into the enormous creature who was now climbing onto the plateau and facing down the bunker.

"He's going to attack!" Yuki shouted just as Ganejin stomped forward and kicked the front wall of the structure with all his might, shattering the concrete face and sending debris flying in every direction.

No sooner had the blow been stricken, a sound not unlike the artillery cannon they had encountered in the desert base cracked through the mountain air before a shell hit Ganejin square in the face, exploding on impact. The weapon didn't appear to cause any real damage, but the smoke disoriented him long enough that a second shell strike in the back on his knee caused him to lose balance and career over the side of the plateau.

"Aw, shit," muttered Yata, half breathless.

"Everybody hang on!" Ivan yelled.

The loud popping of artillery being fired and missing their target sounded around them as Alkonoth launched herself off the peak and landed on the plateau in one blindingly fast motion. As soon as she felt the impact of the bird's foot on the ground, Yuki pushed herself off of it and barrel rolled out of the way. Ivan and Yata followed the same motion, while Manny threw himself backwards, landing on his right arm with an excruciating snap.

Yata rushed to him to look at his arm, holding it up to reveal that it had been forced backwards at the elbow, the boy's radius sticking straight out of the skin as his entire forearm hung limp. Manny didn't make a sound, instead staring at his fractured appendage in silent shock. Yuki looked on in horror for a moment before the sound and flying dirt from a nearby explosion rocked her back to her senses.

"We have to keep moving," she shouted, "into the bunker!"

"Look at him!" screamed Yata, visibly upset. "He's just a kid!"

"No," Manny coughed, "I can make it. If we find the amulets, my arm is fixed. No use sitting here."

With an expression of surprise at the boy's resilience, Yata nodded and helped him to his feet. Yuki looked up to see Alkonoth standing behind them, wings outstretched to shield them from oncoming cannon fire. The bird looked over its shoulder and squawked urgently, a signal that they had to move. On the other side of the plateau, Ganejin's hand reached over the edge as he pulled himself out of the crevasse, explosions impacting all over him.

"They're giving us a chance," Yuki commanded, "let's go!"

The four of them, Yuki in front while Ivan and Yata carried Manny by the shoulders, scampered away from the battle and into the gaping hole that Ganejin had bashed into the front of the bunker. Inside they found a deserted barracks, the soldiers no doubt evacuated into the interior.

Rifles lay hung up on a long rack in the middle of the otherwise empty concrete room. Yuki almost grabbed one, immediately flashing back to her time in the military. This would be the first time since that fateful battle that she would have held a weapon of any kind, let alone a Laurentian rifle.

"Do you guys want one of these?" she asked her companions.

"We've got our hands full," Yata replied, nodding toward Manny, who was now breathing heavily. "You'll just have to do all the fighting for us."

Taking a deep breath, she picked up the weapon and loaded it before proceeding cautiously toward the door at the end of the room.

The door appeared to be heavily fortified, but had been left slightly ajar in what had surely been a mad rush to get out of the way of Ganejin's foot. Gently, she pushed it open. Its metal hinges made a slight squeaking sound as it moved, but nothing loud enough to give away their position. Before her was a bare concrete hallway, dimly lit with what appeared to be gas lamps. She looked back over her shoulder to the three men, all looking apprehensive, and gave a hand signal to follow her.

The only sounds she could hear as she moved through the hall were the slight footsteps and heavy breathing of her team. About five meters ahead, the hallway branched out into a side corridor. A small sniffling noise seemed to be emanating from it. Holding up her hand, she signaled for her followers to stop. Exhaling, she drew her weapon into firing position and stepped around the corner.

The nose of her rifle jammed into the forehead of a Laurentian officer crouching on the ground. Yuki's finger wavered on the trigger, ready to paint the walls with the inside of his head, until she realized he was unarmed.

"Don't move!" she yelled frantically, adrenaline rushing through her.

The man had a slight, non-intimidating figure and it appeared that he wasn't prepared at all for combat.

"I didn't know there would be ground troops," he said sheepishly, his face contorting into a vaguely sinister smile.

"Take us to where you're keeping the amulets." Yuki demanded harshly, not wanting to waste any time.

"And why should I do that," the man snapped back

"Tell me where they are or I'll kill you," she barked.

"Go ahead," he taunted, "not much longer anyway."

Confounded and disgusted, Yuki moved the barrel of the gun from his head to his right hand and pulled the trigger. An explosion of carnal viscera blasted through the middle of his palm, sending chunks of flesh and finger bones flying in every direction. His smile disappeared as he screeched in agony, holding up the bleeding appendage.

"Holy shit, Yuki," Yata gagged in horror.

She felt a tinge of unease at acting on her violent impulse, but there was no going back.

"Well then, I'll keep making your last moments hell," she roared with demonic fury, jabbing the rifle barrel into the crotch of his pants, "unless you tell me where they are."

"S-something came in t-today," the wounded man stuttered. "A box from the LCC."

"Just show us."

"Alright," he said, "alright."

The five of them crammed themselves into an elevator at the end of the side corridor.

"Fourteen levels down," the officer sniveled, "I'd pull the lever, but..."

Yuki jammed the butt of her rifle into the control that started the elevator, beginning their descent.

"How many levels are in this place?" asked Yata.

"Lots," the man sneered through gritted teeth. "Best one's at the bottom."

Before Yata could ask what was on the bottom level, Yuki jammed the lever back and opened the doors to level fourteen. They stepped out into an even more dimly lit hallway, similarly spartan in décor with the same solid concrete walls.

"To the left," said their guide.

Yuki turned to see a large wooden door with a glass window in the middle. Lifting the butt of her rifle, she smashed the glass and reached through, turning the lock from the other side and pushing to door open. Inside was a large, dark room filled with small tables covered in messes of papers and assorted trash. Her eyes scanned for any sign of the amulets, landing on a wooden crate atop the farthest table.

"Is that it?" she demanded, pointing to it.

Rather than respond, he looked down at his hand, still wincing in pain.

Frantically she vaulted over the tables, banging her knee in the process. She leapt onto the crate, hacking into the wooden panels with the butt of her rifle and tearing them up when they were loosened. Reaching inside, she exhaled as a smile came across her face, her fingers grasping the large jade amulet of Ganejin. Pulling it out and tucking it under her arm, she retrieved Alkonoth's golden pendant and Jhalaragon's carved stone. At last she felt her fingers enclose around the all-too-familiar amulet of Narajin.

Yuki, hurry!

It was the first time in more than a day that she had heard Narajin's voice in her head. It was a welcome embrace to hear him again, but there was something about the urgency in his tone that made her think something was wrong.

"Ok," she asserted, running back to her companions, "let's do this."

As she handed the amulets back to their rightful owners, a ringing noise blared through the room, followed by another sound, even more unwelcome.

"*Hello my friends!*" Houston's voice echoed off the concrete walls, sounding tinny and crackling with static. "*I figured you might come lookin' for your stuff, which is why I thought... You know where the best possible place to stash 'em would be? Right here, home of my real masterpiece. Ooh, you're gonna love this one! You've got the best seats in the house to enjoy my big reveal!*"

"You fucker," Ivan muttered under his breath.

"*When your big dumb friends knocked on the door,*" Houston's voice continued, "*they lit a fuse.*"

A chill ran up Yuki's spine as her greatest fears were confirmed.

"*It'll be a demonstration for the world to see. If we can't control the kaiju, we'll kill 'em!*"

"You can't," Manny retorted, despite the recorded nature of Houston's message, "it's impossible!"

"*It's time to show the world that even the gods can die.*"

"What the hell is he talking about?" Yata exclaimed. "What's gonna happen?"

"What he means," said their injured guide, still slouching in the doorway but now wearing a sinister grin, "is that about... one minute from now, the timer is gonna reach zero, and it's gonna detonate a bomb. It'll destroy this compound, and unleash a force unlike anything you've ever imagined."

"Get out of here," Yuki screamed to her friends, "now!"

Light and colors swirled through Yuki's vision as she changed form and place, returning to a familiar presence.

Yuki, what is wrong?

The bomb. Atom fire. It's in the base.

Narajin fell silent for a moment. Yuki took the time to gain awareness of their location, just over a kilometer beyond the plateau overlooking it from a mountaintop.

It will not kill us, Narajin said at last, *but that it exists might mean that the Pantheon has failed – and what comes next will surely kill us all.*

No, no, none of that! Yuki reprimanded him.

She watched as Alkonoth took flight and Jhalaragon and Ganejin jumped over the side of the plateau, no doubt running from the oncoming explosion.

We have come to this at last, Narajin intoned sorrowfully, *ending where we began.*

No, what is that? We're gonna keep fighting!

We will fight whatever comes our way, Yuki, but this fight may be our last. I have enjoyed having you as my friend.

Narajin's words were a heavy blow to the heart. He was her friend, and seeing him in this deep of despair shook her to the core.

I've enjoyed having you as my friend, too, you big old cat.

The plateau burst and a ball of light blazed forth, brighter than the sun, enveloping all before it. It was great and terrible, unlike anything Yuki had ever seen. The shockwave hit harder than the erupting volcano in Tarakona, the smoke and debris thicker than the destruction of the desert.

When Narajin's eyes adjusted and the smoke left their field of vision, she saw it – the mushroom cloud, rising from a gaping wound in the surface of the world between the shattered mountains.

Bits of fiery, radioactive debris rained down from the cloud like bright golden leaves falling from a monstrous tree. The autumn of the Earth had arrived, and winter would be left in its wake.

Chapter 16:
The New Kaiju

A horrible guttural sound belched from the pillar of radioactive smoke, echoing off of the demolished mountains around it. The voice was far less animalistic than the battle cries of the Pantheon, but its cadence was warped and unnatural, more a tortured wail than a vocalization of challenge.

Ww... Yuki stammered, having momentarily lost the ability to construct words, *what...*

Silence and stillness followed for another ten seconds before the sound returned. It clearly emanated from a living creature, but not like any Yuki had ever heard – frightened but filled with uncontrollable hatred, feral beyond madness, tormented by its very existence.

It would seem, Narajin said, his voice nearly trembling, *that we are no longer alone.*

A quick flash of green light within the mushroom cloud backlit an enormous, contorted shape. It almost appeared to be a giant animal, unnaturally thin and severely hunched forward. Its broad shoulders hung at the same relative height as its head, perched atop a slender body with four long, spider-like limbs.

The surface of the cloud column shifted as an elongated finger with charred, dark blue skin reached out of its atomic cocoon and into the world. Slowly and purposefully it moved up and down, as if to test the air outside. Its skin cracked and sizzled as it contacted the air, jets of steam pouring off of it. A third wail sounded as a towering, slender leg stepped out and impacted the ground.

At last the cloud burst open and revealed its face, misshapen and demonic. The creature's asymmetry was revolting, a convulsing mess of facial features smeared across the front of a bulbous head. Its wide, skeletal grin hung propped open by gigantic knife-like fangs that seemed too big to fit inside. Massive eye sockets sloped inwards to beady, lidless eyeballs that hung in their indented centers. Smoke from the mushroom cloud rolled off of it as it stood, peering malevolently out at the world into which it had been birthed.

What the fuck is that thing? Yuki gasped.

A new kaiju, Narajin replied.

Can we... I don't know, talk to it? Tell it we're friends or something?

It is an antibody attacking a disease, born into this world to do one thing – finish what we could not.

Ok... Well, there's four of us and one of it.

The creature's unblinking eyes stopped scanning and locked eyes with them.

I have never seen a kaiju like this before, Narajin intoned.

The nightmare beast screamed once more. In one swift movement, it lunged toward them at an impossible speed, arms outstretched and radioactive saliva flying from its unhinged mouth. One thought surged through Yuki's mind, the only thing about this creature that was abundantly clear – it wanted to eat them.

Without hesitating, Yuki and Narajin crouched into a fighting stance. The mutant kaiju leapt across the ravine and landed on the rock face just below them, scrambling spastically to avoid falling down the cliff face before digging into the rock with its teeth and pulling itself up toward them.

Not a chance, Yuki taunted.

Preparing to stomp on its face and send it tumbling back down the side of the mountain, Yuki's enthusiasm was cut short when the monster dodged Narajin's right foot and swiped at their left leg with its razor-sharp claws, knocking them over backwards.

Before they could right themselves, the creature pounced on top of them and sunk its disproportionately massive teeth into their chest, pulling its head back and ripping out a huge chunk of flesh that it proceeded to gag on for a moment before swallowing it whole.

Yuki screamed in agony, blood pouring out of Narajin's gaping chest wound.

Yuki, focus! he commanded.

As the hell beast reared back to take another bite, they jammed their left fist straight into its throat. The creature gagged and coughed up some pieces of Narajin's flesh that were still making their way down, sprinkling them with regurgitated shreds of their own body.

The sky darkened, a shadow passing over the two battling monsters as a third joined the fray. Talons outstretched, Alkonoth landed on the new creature's shoulders and dug in until green blood poured forth from the puncture wounds. Flapping their wings, the bird kaiju tried to lift the monster off of Narajin, but the newcomer wrapped its arms around them and held on, taking the three kaiju airborne as Yuki and Narajin clamped down both of their claws on their attacker's jaws to prevent it from taking another bite. Straining to keep aloft, the combined weight quickly proved too much for the bird as the three entangled monsters soon plummeted earthward into a crevasse next to what remained of the plateau.

The three kaiju slammed and ricochetted against the sides of the ravine as they fell, Alkonoth flapping and squawking furiously as Narajin wrestled with trying to keep the new predatory monster's mouth shut. A violent crash caused Yuki to lose focus and let go, allowing the creature to open its mouth and roar, sending more regurgitated flesh chunks flying into their face. Suddenly, a massive fist pummeled the monster in the face. It was Ganejin, who had apparently been climbing up out of the ravine when the other kaiju toppled onto him.

Manny, she exclaimed exasperatedly, *thanks for joining us.*

My pleasure, he responded while accidentally kneeing Narajin in the head as the four monsters plunged toward the ground.

Finally they crashed into a heap on the floor of the ravine. Ganejin landed on the bottom, somewhat cushioning the impact, but that was somewhat nullified by Alkonoth and the new creature sandwiching them in between. Yuki looked up to see Jhalaragon trotting over, tongue snaking in and out of his mouth.

What the hell happened? Yata asked, sounding bewildered. *What... What's that thing?*

No sooner had he spoken then the beast jerked back into consciousness, snapping its jaws wildly as Narajin's blood still dripped from its fangs. Before it could take another bite, Yuki jammed their knee into its side and rolled over, sending it toppling onto the ground where it scampered for a moment before righting itself and, seeing that Jhalaragon was the closest, jumped on him and sank its teeth into the side of his neck. Stunned, the reptile tried to free itself, whipping his tail against his attacker, the creature still holding its relentless, vice-like grip.

Pushing himself off the ground once the other kaiju had cleared off of him, Ganejin finally righted himself and lunged at the grappling beasts, pummeling the newcomer with two of his fists and forcing it to let go of its prey. The foul beast turned around just in time for another of the elephant's fists to slam straight into its forehead while another grabbed its left arm.

Not wanting to be left out of what seemed to be the final tussle with this thing, Yuki and Narajin sprang forward and sunk both of their claws into the creature's torso opposite Ganejin, who was beginning to pull the thing's arm away from them. Yuki caught on to what he was trying to do and began pulling its body in the opposite direction until a ripping sound filled the air. Skin tore and tendons snapped as the monster's right arm separated from its body.

The beast howled in pain, shaking violently as green blood poured from its shoulder socket. Unable to stop at dismemberment, Ganejin began beating the creature over the head with its own arm as its throes of pain quickly turned to intense rage. In a crazed, almost suicidal motion, it launched itself at the elephant monster teeth first, slashing him across the face and causing him to screech and stop the attack long enough for it to escape up the side of the cliff face on its three remaining limbs.

At this point the creature almost seemed pitiful, until Yuki looked around and realized that it had dealt just as much damage to the Pantheon as they had to it. Jhalaragon lay on his side nursing his throat wound, while Alkonoth held their left wing outstretched, having torn it during the fall. It took her a moment to remember that they too were leaking blood out of the sizable hole in their chest.

The mushroom cloud still rose ominously above them as the creature climbed towards it, as if returning to the womb from whence it was birthed minutes before. As it reached the edge of the rock face, another rumble sounded, this time much heavier than that made by the creature's footsteps. The deformed beast stopped in its tracks as frightened and unsure of what was coming as the rest of them.

A massive hand, larger than even Ganejin's, emerged from the smoke and slammed itself down on the rocks. The cloud burst and a hideous being emerged, as vaguely humanoid in shape as the first monster but much more muscularly built. It featured the same elongated head, its loose-hanging jaw giving it the appearance of a malevolent sneer as it glared out at its audience through almost human eyes.

The smaller creature screamed as the new beast's hand pushed its head to the ground, the larger monster shifting its weight forward to pull itself out of the crater. The first creature's screams cut short when its skull smashed under the new adversary's palm. The beast fully emerged to the cliff's edge and roared a challenge to the Pantheon, syrupy, green blood and fragments of calvarium raining from its fingers.

No... deadpanned Yata.

Standing at the edge for a long moment, the gargantuan monster stared down the kaiju below it. Gradually, Yuki noticed the red glow in its eyes building in intensity.

I... I think something's gonna happen, she warned, *I think we should –*

A tremendous blast of red plasma burst from the monster's unhinged mouth and bathed the kaiju in its explosive, fiery barrage. Narajin's fur singed and caught flame as Yuki winced at the burning sensation washing over them. Inadvertently, the attack had cauterized their chest wound and stopped the bleeding, but it had still done significant damage itself.

Yuki felt weak as the plasma bolts rained down on them, her vision beginning to cloud. They didn't have the strength to fire back, move out of the way, or even stand. The barrage was relentless, draining every drop of energy that remained in them until there was next to nothing left.

I don't think I can summon a volcano this time, she thought.

We are not alone, Yuki. As you said yourself, there is only one of it, and four of us.

But how –

Call to them.

In her mind, she reached for any traces of Manny, Yata, and Ivan that she could find. They were taking as much of a beating as she was – she would have to find a way to get through it.

Unless that was the answer. Through their adventure, the four companions had shared in suffering, both physical and psychological, at the hands of the enemy. It was a common thread that would always be a part of them – but it didn't destroy them, it bound them to each other.

One by one, the memories came flooding back. She could feel the pain of each of her friends – but rather than making her feel desolation, it made her want to fight back. That they had all shared the experiences together made her feel like she *could* fight back. There was nothing they hadn't yet overcome.

Just keep going.

Mana surged through the Pantheon, their life forces inexorably linked. Fatigue turned to strength, senses cleared, and one by one, they stood up. Red plasma lightning continued to dance over them, but its destructive power had little affect as each of the monsters took their fighting stance. Alkonoth held their wings aloft, head reared back. Ganejin raised his four fists, lightening beginning to charge along his knuckles. Jhalaragon opened his frill, roaring in challenge. Narajin, and Yuki, crouched with one arm behind their head and another outstretched forward, ready to meet the enemy, fire building inside of them.

The monster standing on the cliff above them, its immense figure framed by the dwindling mushroom cloud, seemed to shift back, unsure of what was about to happen.

Yuki tried to think of something inspiring to say, but all that filled her head was pure adrenaline. She belted out a blood-curdling scream to the others, who soon joined in with animalistic war cries of their own. At once, they released their attacks – Narajin's plasma fireball rocketed upwards as Ganejin's lightening entangled the attacking beast. Jhalaragon jetted a stream of liquid flame from his mouth, while Alkonoth spat a concentrated energy beam – abilities that had lain dormant now brought to the surface.

The top of the cliff where the monster stood exploded in a wall of fire and electricity. The monster's attack stopped, but it remained standing, digging its feet into the ground to take the impact of the blasts.

Not waiting for it to gain control of itself again, Narajin bounded up the side of the cliff face, flanked by Jhalaragon as Alkonoth picked up Ganejin and flew upwards. Yuki vaulted over the precipice of the ravine and jumped into a spin mid-air, landing a roundhouse kick on the side of the monster's head.

Having ascended a kilometer directly over them, Alkonoth let go of Ganejin, whose body surged with lightening as he descended. The elephant god smashed onto the enemy combatant with the force of an impacting asteroid, an explosion of electricity oscillating around them.

When the debris cleared and Ganejin had stood up, the hulking destroyer lay incapacitated and seemingly unconscious. Not one to take chances, Jhalaragon ran up and torched its entire body with liquid fire. Flames enveloped the creature, dancing across its skin as it became a gargantuan pyre.

Hell yeah! Manny shouted, a sentiment they all shared.

The four kaiju together, harnessing the power of the Earth, had proven more powerful than anything a single abomination could throw at them. Ganejin beat his chest in triumph, sounding a loud trumpet that echoed through the mountains, announcing their victory.

Her gaze drifting across the mountain tops, Yuki enjoyed a rare moment of tranquility. There wasn't anyone attacking them, they weren't being chased, and they had stopped the immediate threat to the world. There might be other bombs, and that would require investigation, but for now the threat was gone.

Unfortunately, the tranquility was short-lived when her eyes landed on something she did not expect to see. Perched atop a peak no more than five kilometers away was a massive, dark figure. There it sat, clad in black fur, peering at them like a specter of death watching an unsuspecting victim. Her eyes locked with its, prompting it to rear back and bellow, grabbing the attention of the rest of the kaiju. There they stood, stricken with fear at the creature that faced them once again – Mokwa.

Chapter 17:

Flight of the Monsters

I knew it would not take long to draw her out, said Narajin.

The bear perched motionless atop the mountain peak staring back at them. It was unclear how much of the battle she had seen, but it was clear that she had decided to take part only as a spectator, as if the kaiju had been fighting for the right to be killed by her afterward.

How long until she comes over here? Ivan asked rhetorically. *I'm sick of waiting.*

I don't know, man, Yata answered, *I'm not sure I want to stop living yet.*

Oh, come on, Yuki snapped at them, pointing to the burning kaiju carcass around which they stood. *We finished off that thing. She's just one more.*

You do not know Mokwa like I do, said Ivan.

Not convinced, Yuki turned back to their steadfast onlooker. It was beginning to seem like Mokwa – or whomever commanded her – was taunting them. The sides of her tremendous body expanded and contracted with slow, steady breaths. Her eyes never moved or blinked, remaining transfixed on the Pantheon's location. Yuki felt like it was her the beast was singling out, but she was too far to know for certain. If it was psychological warfare in which Mokwa was engaging them, she was winning.

CRACK.

The flaming carcass in front of them shook as the sound of splitting bones echoed from it. Jhalaragon leapt backwards, the others' faces frozen in shock at their slain enemy showing any sign of movement.

Now what, said Yata, his breath trembling. A second, longer cracking sound began, the chest of the lifeless creature warping and buckling as something pushed against it from the other side. A sharp, bony protrusion ripped upwards through the sternum and sliced down the center of the torso, splitting open the body cavity and throwing green slime outwards at the kaiju. The appendage reached into the air, unfurling into a skeletal wing covered in armored bone with thick membranes stretched between the long bat-like fingers. A second wing burst forth next to it, causing another slime explosion and further ripping open the body.

The creature's face collapsed inward as the inside of its head withdrew like a cicada shedding its skin. Out of the flaming shell of a carcass the beast arose once more, reborn from the flames and dripping in its own afterbirth. Still vaguely humanoid with the same horrible face, it was now clad in a rocky exoskeleton with the two enormous wings folded under its arms.

Staring aghast at the hideous sight, the Pantheon barely had time to react before the monster lashed out with a blast from its ray. Red plasma danced across Yuki's field of vision, momentarily blinding her until something gigantic knocked them on the back of the head as it catapulted over them. A moment later, the energy assault was cut short as Mokwa burst onto the plateau and began grappling with the mammoth gargoyle amidst the flames between them. Unsure of who to attack, the Pantheon unleashed their projectile breath weapons in unison, pelting the wrestling beasts with a storm of napalm, lasers, and plasma.

Their melee didn't last long before the demon flapped open its wings and beat them furiously, trying to flee into the air and knocking the Pantheon backwards with the hurricane force winds. Mokwa dug her claws into its body and held on as it took flight.

Not wanting either of them to escape, Ganejin grabbed onto Mokwa just before they ascended out of reach. Together the three kaiju sailed north over the mountains, bobbing and weaving as the gargoyle tried to shake off the other two.

Quick, Ivan commanded as Alkonoth lifted off the ground, *before they get away!*

I'll catch up on foot, said Yata just before Jhalaragon launched himself northward, his reptilian limbs catapulting them over the rocky landscape.

I guess we're with you again, Yuki said to Ivan as Alkonoth grabbed Narajin by the shoulders. *Let's go get 'em.*

Yuki was surprised at how much she had gotten used to being dragged through the air by the monster and host that had previously tried to kill them. Of course, that was before she had seen that his drive to fight came from a place similar to hers. Now that they had found a common enemy and had no reason to be at each other's throats, she had experienced just how loyally he would defend those who called him an ally.

Hey, Ivan, she said, *let's aim for the demon thing – the one with the wings – we'll have a better chance of joining the rumble if we shoot them down.*

No sooner had the words left her mind but Alkonoth's powerful energy beam blazed out of their mouth and extended far into the distance. It brushed against the beast's right wing, sparks flying from the contact but not causing enough damage to bring it down. Closing their eyes and drawing all of their energy inward, Yuki and Narajin exhaled and fired a plasma bolt, missing their target and striking Mokwa instead, the bear bellowing with rage but unable to turn around and fire back.

We'll have to get closer! Yuki yelled.

I am going as fast as I can! Ivan retorted.

Apparently frustrated by not being able to launch a counterattack, Mokwa took out her rage on Ganejin, blasting the elephant in the face with her energy beam as he howled, dangling precariously below the other two monsters.

Through the night they flew, keeping all eyes on the fleeing monsters. As the sun began to rise again in the East, Yuki noticed that they were no longer over the mountains, but a sprawling plain of yellow grass stretching beneath them. A great, vast forest began to the east, and on the northern horizon arose the rectangular mountains of a ruined old world city.

It must be fleeing to the ruins, said Ivan, *it thinks it can evade us in there.*

Nice try, said Yuki, summoning the power for another long-range attack.

This time, Narajin's plasma bolt found its mark, grazing the gargoyle's wing and ripping the membrane that kept it aloft. The monster's flight wavered as they began to lose altitude, weighed down by the two monsters snapping and swatting at each other beneath it.

As hours passed and the sun traveled most of its way westward across the sky, the monoliths of the old civilization drew nearer, overgrown with vegetation from their return to the natural world around them. The life energy of this place was palpable, the land seeming to emit mana and send it coursing through Yuki's veins.

Just a little further, Ivan – just over those buildings. Then we've got 'em!

They didn't even have to fire another shot as Ganejin sent waves of electric discharge surging through Mokwa's body and into the already-struggling gargoyle, causing it to completely lose its equilibrium. Plummeting toward the ruined city, Mokwa yanked on the formerly-flying monster and sent it careening into Ganejin as they disappeared into the steel canyons.

There, said Yuki, *take us in!*

You've got it, Ivan spat back, *hold on!*

Alkonoth dove toward the city, holding Narajin until they reached about four hundred meters from the top of the nearest building, then letting go and sending Yuki plunging downward. Wind howled past their ears as they dropped toward the battle's arena, an exhilarating sensation punctuated by the impact of their feet hitting the top of the building.

Still about a kilometer off the ground, they sprinted forward, bounding from one rooftop to the next, caving in the top floors of buildings that had stood abandoned for over five thousand years. Overgrown grass and trees crunched underfoot as they crossed the structures toward the spot where the three other monsters fell.

Through the twilight on the other side of the city, Yuki could see the shore of a lake. Somehow it felt slightly familiar, a feeling a deja-vu momentarily distracting her before the sound of Ganejin's trumpet snapped her attention back to the task at hand.

A heavy rumbling noise filled the air as an especially tall spire-like building a few blocks to the north began to topple over, providing a visual indicator of where the battle was taking place. The dust cloud raised by the collapsing building swirled violently as the debris was stirred up and flung in every direction by the savage bout going on within.

Narajin leapt toward the three-way free-for-all, trying to single out the individual monsters so as not to attack their ally, but the swirling gray-brown cloud around them made distinguishing any details immensely difficult. Deciding to jump right in and hope for the best, they collided in mid-air with Ganejin, both catapulting backwards away from the ominous silhouette of Mokwa grappling with the winged gargoyle, backlit by surging red and green plasma blasts.

Yuki, shouted Manny, *you caught up with us!*

She didn't even have time to reply as Mokwa tossed the gargoyle out of the wall of debris at them, striking Ganejin head-on. The great elephant rolled backwards, grappling the hell beast with all four arms and unleashing a torrent of electricity through its body.

With Ganejin's hands full, Yuki and Narajin found themselves staring alone into the eyes of Mokwa for the first time since Tarakona. Smoke flared from the bear's nostrils as it stepped forward, gaining momentum with each stride. Narajin charged up a plasma bolt and fired, igniting the fur on Mokwa's left shoulder. Barely noticing, the living mountain kept barreling forward toward them.

Just before she reached them, a metallic crash sounded as Alkonoth rammed into the top half of a building next to them and sent it careening to the ground, landing square on top of the charging bear. Narajin took the opportunity to find higher ground, clamoring up the side of an adjacent skyscraper as Mokwa, not losing her momentum, exploded out of the collapsing debris and skidded to a halt just below them. Stopped in her tracks momentarily, she looked up and sounded a roar to let them know she was coming.

Hovering above, Alkonoth fired their ray at her as Narajin climbed to the relative safety of a rooftop. Enraged, Mokwa charged head-first into the base of the building, demolishing the foundation. Yuki and Narajin struggled to keep their balance as the rooftop gave way and the edifice crumbled.

Ivan, yelled Yuki, *now would be a good time to –*

Before she could finish, they were away, the building crumbling below them as they lifted into the sky. As they drifted away from the chaos and toward the shore, Yuki found herself once more transfixed by the water. It wasn't her first time seeing it, but she had no idea where else she would have. It appeared almost as big as an ocean, but as far as she knew they were still inland, and the curvature of the shoreline indicated that it was in fact a giant lake.

Her pondering was once again interrupted by the sudden impact above them. The gargoyle had managed to escape Ganejin and had collided with Alkonoth. The bird squawked and screeched as the thing ripped into their flesh. Their flight trajectory began to dip toward the lakefront.

As the tops of the buildings loomed close, Yuki reached out and grabbed onto a tower with two thin spires mounted on the roof. It was much too thin to support the weight of a kaiju and crumbled instantly, but Narajin grabbed one of the spires and ripped it out of its foundation before flipping over backwards to land on their feet just out of range of the destruction, holding the structural point like a spear.

A loud crash and a rumble in the earth signaled that the two aerial monsters had landed just to the east. Yuki and Narajin turned and ran toward the sound, weapon in hand, smashing over and through any structure that stood in their way.

When they cleared the final row of buildings, Yuki found herself looking out at the lakeshore. Between her and it was the gargoyle, looming over Alkonoth with one foot on the ibis' left wing while the other prepared to stomp on their head.

Not wasting a moment, Yuki and Narajin charged forward, spire outstretched, and impaled it through the beast's chest. The monster staggered backwards howling in pain, but Yuki did not let go, instead twisting the metal rod and making the wound gush even more of its green blood. A red glint in the monster's eyes told her it was about to charge up its projectile weapon. Without hesitation, Yuki stepped backward, pulling the spire out of the monster's torso and drawing it back before swinging it with all their strength at the creature's neck. The metal tore through the flesh but snapped in half at the spinal column, unable to break through the bone.

Blood gushed out of the monster's nearly-cleaved neck, arteries spraying green syrup like geysers as its head convulsed and struggled to remain attached to its body. Plasma continued to build behind its eyes as Yuki and Narajin's minds whirred together, trying to beat it to its attack.

Diving to the ground, they picked up the two shards of the spire in each hand.

Ohoho... she laughed, realizing her and Narajin's strategy as they stood back, facing the Gargoyle head on.

Boy have I got something to show you, Yuki spat towards the mutant abomination, drawing the metal rods back over their shoulders and crouching into an attack position. *Watch this!*

In a single motion, they lunged forward toward its face, jamming the enormous spears as hard as they could through the beast's eyeballs. Twisting and forcing them further inward, she felt it beginning to lose control of its energy discharge as plasma bolts danced in chaos across its face.

They jumped backwards, the creature emitting a blood-curdling wail as its plasma enveloped the metal spikes in a dazzling array of red light that lit up their surroundings. Watching their enemy succumb to its own still-intensifying attack, Yuki blurted out the first four words that entered her mind.

It's time to party.

The hideous beast let out one final scream moments before its head blasted apart in an eruption of crimson energy, emerald blood, and shattered skull fragments that flew in every direction, spraying the sides of buildings and dousing the vicinity with roasted, gooey monster viscera.

Yuki and Narajin wiped the creature's blood out of their eyes, revealing its headless body still standing upright, motionless. For fear of it somehow continuing to fight without a head, they took their battle stance, left arm outstretched in front of them in challenge. As if in response, the Gargoyle's decapitated corpse slowly began to topple over backwards. As soon as it touched the ground, it enveloped itself and the surrounding area in a massive, fiery explosion that instantly obliterated whatever was left of it. Alkonoth squawked and stumbled away, flapping out the flames that clung to their wings.

Is that thing finally dead? Ivan asked.

Another explosion blasting what was left of its corpse to even smaller pieces seemed to answer his question. Yuki and Narajin breathed a simultaneous sigh of relief at the vanquishing of their foe.

I have not experienced a fight like that since... Narajin mused.

That's it, Yuki said. *That's the last of them.*

Until next time, said Narajin. *Laurentia may have other bombs waiting to be used.*

Come on, man. Can't we just relax for... I don't know, a minute?

We do not have a minute. Especially when the enemy is still nearby.

The enemy... Oh, right, you mean –

Her thought was interrupted when Mokwa burst from the buildings behind them. They spun around to face her, fear paralyzing Yuki at the realization that they had used up much of their energy defeating the other kaiju and wouldn't last long against the former member of the Pantheon.

They stood, waiting, bracing themselves – but Mokwa didn't attack. Her gaze seemed to be fixed on a point beyond them. Something had completely captivated her attention and was making her stand as motionless as a statue. Something was going on inside her head that had taken precedence even over breathing.

Then Yuki realized what it was – she was staring at the lake. What had seemed familiar to her upon seeing it had now completely overwhelmed the enormous bear in front of them.

What's happening? Yuki asked.

I do not know, Narajin responded. *I have never seen this before.*

An eternity seemed to pass as they stood in the presence of their enemy who minutes before had been trying to kill them, now staring blankly at a body of water, seeming to forget the world around her.

Gradually, the burning light in her eyes began to change. The rage-filled glow that Yuki had come to associate with her seemed to lower in intensity – almost indicating sorrow.

Then, as abruptly as she had joined them, Mokwa turned to her left and began walking, first slowly and then building into a sprint until reaching an all-out run as she made her way down the lakeshore, the sun beginning to rise over the water.

Where is she going? Yuki asked.

I said before, answered Narajin, *I do not know.*

Thundering footsteps to their right announced the arrival of Ganejin.

Hi guys, said Manny, *what did I miss?*

No one answered, their eyes fixed on Mokwa as she bounded away from them.

Is that the other bad one? He asked, pointing to the smoldering pieces of flesh still glowing like burnt embers. *Nice job. Hey, why is she running away?*

We don't know, Manny, Yuki finally responded, *but I think we should follow her and find out.*

Pounding, rapid footfalls drew nearer as Jhalaragon leapt off the top of the nearest skyscraper and landed amidst the monster's burning remains.

Alright, where is it? Yata exclaimed. *Let's kick its ass!*

Look around you, said Ivan, *could've used your help ten minutes ago.*

The reptile scanned the ground, his alert movements becoming weighed down with disappointment.

Well then, he said, *where's Mokwa?*

When none of them answered, he followed their gaze up the shoreline to the shrinking dot that was the fleeing bear kaiju.

Well, come on, he said, *why are we just standing around? Let's go get her!*

With a stomp of his left hind leg, he sprinted after her. Turning to their companions, Yuki shared a moment of silent agreement before they all followed suit.

Down the shoreline they ran, Alkonoth gliding above, the endless city becoming an industrial wasteland overgrown with forrest as they followed the curvature of the lake. Mokwa would occasionally disappear momentarily behind an obstacle, but would always reappear, a distant dot on the horizon, never slowing down or stopping.

Gold and brown leaves covered the ground between the long-abandoned factories. Moss crept up the sides of ancient smokestacks, and small birds flew from the treetops to get out of the way of the kaiju as they barreled through. At last the final smokestack disappeared and they found themselves in a full-blown forest of autumnal maples and giant evergreens standing hundreds of feet high.

It felt untouched by humans or apocalypse, completely regrown in the spirit of the living Earth. It was as beautiful as Narai. More importantly, it reminded Yuki of home.

After hours of running, the sun began to descend toward the lake from whence it came, indicating that they were now to its east. Looking ahead, Yuki noticed that the black dot that was Mokwa had stopped beyond the trees and she sat on a sandy beach overlooking the water.

As they approached, it became clear that she was as motionless as before, staring outward like a statue, fixated on something out in the water. Alkonoth and Jhalaragon reached her first, perching themselves at the tree line overlooking the beach, unsure of what to do next.

Yuki shifted her gaze from Mokwa to the direction in which the bear was looking. Out on the water, backlit by the sun, were two small islands. Instantly, she remembered.

This is it, she said to Narajin, *this is what I saw when I looked into her mind in Tarakona.*

Then this place must be the single thing that shone through of her own mind, he responded.

But why did she remember it? And why did she come back here, unless...

She noticed a small speck in the sand next to where Mokwa sat. At first it looked like a small piece of driftwood, but she soon realized that it was a human.

I think I know who that is, she said. *I'm getting out.*

No, Yuki, it is not safe!

Sorry, buddy, but I've got to find out.

Her human eyes flashed into focus and she found herself standing on the beach in front of Narajin. Looking up over he shoulder, she saw his expression of worried scorn facing her down. She turned back and ran toward the unmoving body. It was a large man in a Laurentian military uniform laying face-down in the sand. When she was alongside him, she reached down and checked his neck for a pulse.

He's alive, she said, clutching her amulet long enough to tell Narajin but not long enough for him to tell her to stop what she was doing.

Turning over the man's unconscious body, she saw exactly what she had expected to see – an amulet hung around his neck. This one appeared to be made of a fossilized tooth the size of her hand with a central indentation in the shape of the smaller tooth. She picked it up and felt a rush of energy and a feeling of pure anguish wash over her, forcing her to let go instantly. She picked up the unconscious man's left hand and found a stone that fit the space on the amulet. Picking it up, she grabbed her own amulet and took it off.

Stop! What are you doing? she could hear Narajin say before she dropped the amulet, cutting him off.

Taking a deep breath, she removed the pendant from around the man's neck and placed it around her own. The wave of sorrow returned, nearly overwhelming every sense. Not waiting another second to think about what she was doing, she placed the stone in its notch on Mokwa's amulet.

Chapter 18:
Song of the Sleeping Bear

A younger Earth, an age of ice.

Cold wind swept over a glacier that unfurled to the horizon. Across it walked a great bear. Young and strong, the harsh elements meant nothing to her – it was the only home she had ever known.

Two small cubs, mere hills next to her mountainous stature, ran and played across the permafrost. Though they strayed from her, she kept them within her sight. There was little that could harm such beasts, but in her the duty as a caring mother she kept a watchful eye.

As dusk settled in, they returned to their home at the edge of the glacier. The great cliff face of pure crystalline ice was not as thick as it once was, but it still provided them with shelter. Tundra stretched to the east, the land of mammoths and humans.

Her two children curling up against her for warmth, she looked out to see a band of tiny humans staring back at her from a distance. To her, they were a marvelous species – ill-fitted for survival but making their lives through adapting. To them, she was a god, the personified embodiment of all nature. They called her Mokwa, the mother of all bears. She cherished their mutual respect and trusted them to keep it.

As the sun rose the next day, her cubs once again ran off the play on the ice, and again she followed. Nothing brought her joy like watching her children enjoy themselves, chasing and wrestling each other but never becoming violent. This was their life together, day after day.

By the time they returned home at sunset, she noticed that the glacier had receded again. Once towering over the landscape, it now rose just above their heads at ground level. She began to worry that eventually it would not provide them shelter, and they would have to find a new home. In the mean time, as long as her children were safe, they would make do.

Upon awakening, she realized that she was alone. Frantically she looked around for her cubs, terrified that something had happened to them. The sound of their reveling on the ice assured her that no such thing had happened.

Getting up to check on them, she noticed that the glacier had again become thinner than ever before. A shame, she thought, that they would soon have to find a new home when her cubs clearly enjoyed this one so much. From the edge of the ice, she watched as they ran circles around each other, far out on the open sheet of frozen water.

Then she heard it. A horrible cracking sound, piercing the crisp air and driving panic into her mind.

The cubs stopped their game and looked around, trying to determine where the sound had come from. She roared to her children, telling them to return, but they seemed intent on examining the source of the noise.

It sounded again, crunching and rumbling as a huge crack formed in front of the cubs. The surface of the ice shifted as if floating on a body of liquid water beneath it. More cracks began to form between what would now clearly become the shore of a lake and the ice flow on which the two young bears now found themselves.

Fear overtook her as she ran toward the edge of the lake, collapsing the ice as soon as she stepped on it. She struggled to right herself just in time to see the ice sheet tip, sending the two cubs falling into the water.

Screaming, she tried to break her way through the ice to get to them. Minutes passed while she struggled, trying to swim to her children, but they did not resurface. At last she found the spot where they had stood. All that was there was broken ice and a bottomless lake.

The great bear swam back to shore and pulled herself out onto the tundra. She tried to piece together the reality of what had happened, but it was impossible. All she loved, all she truly cared about was now gone.

Turning to face the water, she considered giving up and walking into the murky depths never to return. Instead, she lay down on the shore and waited, wondering how nature could be so cruel, how unfeeling the Earth must be to take away her children.

Unable to fathom that they were truly gone, she took it upon herself to wait for their return. Slowly, she drifted to sleep.

The remains of the glacier melted, the age of ice passed, and sand built up along the shore, burying the sleeping bear in a massive dune. The bodies of her dead cubs each built up into small islands out in the lake, across from where their mother lay.

Millennia flashed by, civilizations rose and fell, and humans scampered over the sand unknowing of what lay beneath. Still she slumbered, waiting for her children to reach the shore.

Then, in her sleep, the great bear sensed that all was not well. Starvation, plague, and atomic fire swept across the land and wiped clean the Earth of the empires of humanity as calamitous behemoths arose from the ashes to finish them off. The Earth, not content with taking just her children, was taking humanity as well.

She had known humans in their infancy, and that the selfish mistakes of a few had lead to disaster did not mean that they deserved to die. After nearly fifteen thousand years of mourning, it was time for the sleeping bear to awaken.

The bear could not defeat the armies of death on her own. She would need to find allies amongst their ranks, a group of like-minded warriors to free humanity of their impending demise. The pain of losing her children would never leave her, but the selflessness they had given her would be shared with the world she dreamed of creating. The companions she forged would be her pillars, as she would be for them – the Pantheon Colossi.

Chapter 19:
Pantheon Colossi

She's back! Yuki shouted to Narajin and her companions through his amulet. *It's her!*

Moments before, she had disconnected from Mokwa and dropped to the ground next to the bear kaiju's former captor, a vision of twenty thousand years surging through her head.

I'm coming back in, she said to Narajin. *But first...*

She stooped down to the unconscious man on the ground in front of her. Drawing her hand back, she struck him across the face as hard as she could. The man's eyes flew open and he gasped in terror.

"You're dying," Yuki snarled. "Where are the rest of the bombs?"

The man looked at her, mouth agape.

"Where are they?" she screamed, striking him again.

"The – the LCC!" he stammered. "They're in the LCC! Houston's got the detonators!"

"Thanks," she said, turning and walking away.

"Are you gonna kill me?"

"No, but I have no idea what she'll do. Get the hell out of here."

At that, the man stumbled to his feet and ran down the beach. Almost immediately, a beam of yellow light struck him, turning him to vapor.

I always hated that guy, said Ivan, he and Alkonoth having made quick work of their former fighting partner.

What did you do? Narajin asked as soon as she fused with him once more.

I joined with her. It was all right there. Her life... Her children. They brought her back. The memories overwhelmed the Laurentian's control.

Yuki, Yata interrupted, *what's happening? What's going on?*

Mokwa's back, she answered, *it's really her this time!*

Is that... A good thing?

Narajin roared at the great bear, still standing motionless by the lake. Slowly, the bear turned to face them. The look in her eyes was now that of overwhelming emotion. It truly was the same Mokwa that Yuki had seen in her memories. She let out a bellowing greeting at them, announcing her return. Ganejin, Alkonoth, and Jhalaragon responded with roars of their own, echoing out across the lake.

The Pantheon Colossi is re-formed! said Narajin.

Now let's get back to Laurentian Central Complex, said Yuki.

Why the hell would we want to go back there? Yata asked.

Because, that's where the other bombs are being stored.

Good, grunted Ivan. *I've got something I need to settle with Houston.*

Then let's get to it.

United at last, the Pantheon Colossi set out to the southwest over forest, plains, and mountains. Mokwa led the way, unabated animal fury unleashing itself and driving her after months of total human control. Having helped free her, Yuki knew that the only thing on the great bear's mind was what the Laurentians had hidden away at the center of their city.

Snowy peaks of mountain tops passed beneath them, clouds of ice crystals flying skyward to join their vaporous brethren with every tremendous footfall. Majestic waterfalls and roaring rapids sprayed back the lifesblood of the Earth in the wake if its champions, glinting rainbows arcing across the landscape over which the monsters thundered – the full force of nature given form.

The sun revolved over and under them twice before they saw it – the familiar industrial blight on the desert's flat horizon, the solid metal towers of the LCC. By that point, there was no way the Laurentians hadn't seen a band of five angry kaiju storming across the desert toward the northern face of the city, but they didn't need the element of surprise. She actually liked that Houston and his cohorts knew they were coming. On their last visit, they had been walking in a glass house trying to find a diplomatic means of ending the conflict. This time, all bets were off.

Cannons began sounding from the walls as soon as they entered range. Yuki felt the pops of some of them finding their mark, but the impacts barely distracted her as the monsters approached.

They're not our targets, said Yata. *Right?*

No, said Yuki, clearly voicing what all of them felt. *We're not taking them out.*

Except for one, Ivan growled.

Yuki understood Ivan's clear determination for retribution all too well. It was Houston who had started the war for his own purposes – Houston who had dragged Ivan into it on the wrong side. It was clear that the former pawn in the man's game was now the iron fist of his doom.

Right, she said.

1 kilometer. Sweat flew from Narajin's fur as they ran, both the lion and Yuki focused as one mind, ready for battle.

800 meters. Swooping overhead, Alkonoth careened toward the wall mounts and took out four of the cannons with their claws.

600 meters. Troops stationed in forward positions began to abandon their posts, running into the city to avoid the coming impact.

400. Ganejin dropped to his knuckles to run on all six limbs, increasing his speed and pounding huge craters into the ground as he neared the wall.

200. As two soldiers prepared to fire a wall-mounted cannon, Jhalaragon opened his frill and roared in challenge, frightening them and causing them to turn from their post and run.

100. Yuki could see the walls of the city vibrating and shaking at their foundations from the earth-shattering force of the kaiju tsunami's approach.

50. The crash of Mokwa plowing into the iron barrier rang through the air.

0.

Extending their claws, Narajin jumped onto the face of the wall and dug into the surface, anchoring them in the metal cliff. One claw after another, they began to scale the wall as soldiers fired down at them from above. Ganejin rammed head-first into the base of the wall, shaking several of the soldiers off their feet and sending them fleeing before he started the climb himself.

Jhalaragon leapt onto the massive gate by which they had previously entered the lower levels and hung onto it until the doors ripped off of their hinges and exposed the inner city to the light of day. Roaring at the inhabitants, he sounded a warning understood in any language before ascending toward the city above as the lower-level citizens began to flood out of the gates en masse. Yuki could see a tall young woman with long black braids looking up at the reptilian kaiju with what seemed to be a look of gratitude as she helped an elderly woman escape with her. With the kaiju climbing toward the upper levels, it was a reasonable assumption that the safest place was outside.

Looking up, Yuki could see a large cannon being aimed down Narajin's position. Narrowing their eyes, she focused on the soldiers operating it, roaring at them fiercely and climbing faster toward their post as they scrambled to load the artillery shell. The men looked nervously from the ascending kaiju to their weapon.

At last they managed to load the shell, but they had already lost the race – Yuki reached up and put their paw over the muzzle of the cannon as it fired, causing the explosion to backfire and destroy the machine. The two soldiers fell backwards before scrambling away, frightened beyond anything they had likely encountered.

As they mounted the top of the wall, she could see the other kaiju joining them perched along the city's northern edge, aside from Mokwa who had smashed through the city's lower level and was now making her way toward the middle of the complex. Turning away from the city, she saw that most of the lower level's residents had emptied out into the desert and were running as fast as they could away from the melee. Assured of their survival, she turned back to the other kaiju in time to see Mokwa climbing a heavily fortified tower.

She's going for the bombs, said Ivan. *Manny, go help her. I'm going to Houston, if anyone wants to join me.*

The detonators must be connected through the middle of his tower, added Yuki. *When he realizes his defenses aren't gonna make it...*

I will kill him before he can do that, growled Ivan.

Well then, said Yata, *glad we're all on the same page.*

Wagging his tail in preparation, Jhalaragon leapt from the wall onto the nearest building amidst a cloud of artillery fire as Ganejin dug his knuckles into the roof beneath him and bounded after Mokwa.

Ready to fly one more time? Ivan asked.

Yeah, said Yuki, *let's go.*

The great bird flapped their wings and picked them up by the shoulders. She realized that it could very well be their last flight if Houston was provoked into setting off the warheads.

Gliding over the city and rising toward the central tower, she could see Jhalaragon following their route on foot. Wondering for a moment what he would contribute, she realized that his ascent from below would provide them with a much needed backup plan for stopping the detonation. Quickly the battle below disappeared as they passed through the clouds, revealing the tops of the government towers.

I'm getting out, she announced to Ivan and Narajin.

What? Ivan called out.

If we plow right through it, he'll slam down the detonator in self-defense. I have to stall him until you can get to him, or until Yata does his thing down below.

What is Yata even doing?

Helping. You can help by staying outside.

I'm the only one who can do it!

Ivan's plea for blood was cut short as she materialized on the platform outside Houston's office. The cold blasted around her, drowning out all other sound as she ran to the door. The guards outside had long since fled, leaving it undefended.

With all her might, she threw herself against the door, thudding against it and falling onto her back. Determined, she got up and ran at it again, this time causing it to creak under the momentum of the impact. Once more she drew back and jumped at the door, finally forcing it open and falling onto the cold marble floor of Houston's office.

At his desk on the far side of the round chamber he sat, staring at her as if she was expected. The smiling, controlled demeanor from their last encounter had given way to stern gravity, the look of a man who had never even thought of facing defeat but was now forced to look straight into its eyes. Still, the outward smugness remained a permanent part of his presentation as he glared at the small woman who had just forced her way into the room.

"Hello again," he said, still trying to taunt her through his barely-disguised fear.

"You know why we're here," she said coldly.

"You're here to play savior to the people. Too bad there'll soon be no one left to save."

"Wrong. The people on the lower level escaped, and they're now far away from here."

Houston stared at her for a moment before once again falling back on his primary defense, snickering softly and shaking his head as if she were a child who had said something pitifully naive.

"You think that running a few miles is gonna get them to safety?" he spat. "There's no escaping this city when it goes critical. The armory that your friends are trying to pillage is loaded with seventy five megatons of nuclear explosive. Five bombs, all rigged to this."

He moved his hand to a small button on the left side of his desk and rested his index finger on it.

"Do you know what this is?" he asked slyly.

"Yeah, I know." she spat.

"Then I hope you know why it's here. Why we need the most powerful weapons. It's for a reason, doll. What you're doing is a huge mistake."

What he was saying seemed contrary to everything he had done – instinctually, she was calling it as a bluff.

"Why do you think I've been trying to form a single protective state? See that tower across the way?" he said, motioning his free left hand toward the window overlooking the areal walkway from which she had entered. "That's our observatory. We've got telescopes in there from the last days of the old world, ones that can see all the way out. Couple years ago... we saw some stuff you just wouldn't believe. That's what all this is for. Gettin' us ready. And if we can't..."

The fear in his eyes grew more apparent than ever, his strange words sending waves of confusion and dread through Yuki's mind. It could've simply been an elaborate last ditch attempt at sympathy. At the moment, that's all she had time to consider.

"Even if that's true," she said, "this is not the way to deal with it."

"Trust me," he replied, his tone lower as his finger trembled on the button. "This is better than what's coming."

A massive tremor shook the room accompanied by the sound of ripping metal below them. A wave of relief washed over Yuki when she heard it, knowing that Yata and Jhalaragon had reached their objective.

"Not this time," she said.

"Oh yeah?" the now visibly terrified man spat incredulously. "How are you gonna manage that?"

"For starters, our friend the island man just ripped out the cables connecting your detonator."

Slowly, his brow furled, as if he didn't understand what she was saying. Then his eyes began to grow wider and his gaze shifted to the button. Taking a deep breath, he hesitated for a second, then closed his eyes and pressed it.

Nothing happened. The sounds of the battle and Jhalaragon's roar continued to drift in from down below. Again, Houston jammed his finger down on the button. Nothing. Frantically he pressed it over and over, still having no reaction. At last, he looked up, confused and more frightened than ever before, tears beginning to stream down his cheeks as he looked at Yuki. His face was that of a small, frightened child who, for the first time in his life, was not getting his way.

"Time's up," she said to him, putting her hand on her amulet.

He's all yours, Ivan, she thought.

The sound of enormous wings getting airborne sounded as a gust of wind blew in through the open door. Houston stood up and backed away from his desk, the dream that he had constructed for himself to rule crumbling around him. Looking around as if trying to find a safe place to hide, he backed up against the window, unbeknownst of the fact that Alkonoth's gigantic face hovered just outside.

The beak of the giant ibis smashed through the glass, impaling Houston through the center of his back. The man stared straight ahead, locking eyes with Yuki as she winced. A look of shock and fear was ingrained on his face as he drew short breaths, still trying to hold onto life with all of his being.

Then Alkonoth began to slowly open their jaws.

Still skewered on the tip of the bird's beak, Houston howled in agony as blood spurted from his mouth. A ripping noise filled the room, the dictator's finely tailored shirt shredding midway and exposing the skin of his stomach as a laceration formed across it from the strain. With a revolting pop of snapping tendons, his abdomen tore open, bathing the area behind his desk in blood and viscera.

Alkonoth pulled their head back out the window just in time for Houston's body to sever and fly apart. For an instant, the Chief Executive's terrified, pained expression held in midair, organs spraying outward in every direction, the Scythian kaiju letting out a victorious squawk. One after the other, the pieces of the felled tyrant dropped from the aperture's view and into the clouds below.

It's over, then, Yuki said to Narajin, voice shaking.

It is, he said.

Blood, entrails, debris, and bodily fluids ran across the crushed marble, a powerful, icy wind blowing through the gaping hole in the wall. Still trembling, she let out a strong exhale and placed her stone into the amulet.

She found herself in Narajin's body, looking down the dizzying height of the tower as they hung onto the side just below Houston's office. Holding firmly, the lion kaiju began to climb down, passing into the cloud layer.

It felt refreshing after the horror she had just seen to be completely immersed in the clouds, unable to see more than a meter or so in front of them. The water sprites danced across their fur, recharging them, strengthening them. After what had nearly been a cataclysm of final death for the planet, nothing was more comforting than knowing that life was still here.

The cloud cover broke beneath them, and below they could see Mokwa making her way steadily down a broad walkway, followed by Ganejin carrying the five warheads in his arms as they headed towards the edge of the city. Behind them, Jhalaragon faced to the rear, hissing and flaring his frill to ward off any who would attempt pursuit. The soldiers had stopped shooting out of fear of the bombs, seemingly shocked that they had been hidden within the city itself, frozen in place as the realization that the battle had been lost seemed to sink in.

Out of the clouds swooped Alkonoth, squawking for the other kaiju's attention. Ganejin looked up just in time for the bird to grab him by the shoulders and lift him and the bombs into the air and out of the city limits.

The surrounding Laurentian soldiers looked on stupefied as the bombs disappeared outside the walls in the hands of two kaiju. The remaining members of the pantheon stopped where they were and looked around at the troops. The humans stared back at them for a moment until Mokwa roared ferociously, sending a clear message – the war was over. One by one, they began putting down their guns and stepping away from their cannons.

So is Houston dead? Yata asked.

Yeah, Yuki replied, *thanks to your help.*

Her voice still wavered slightly, shaken by the violent image of their enemy's demise – and by something else.

Did... she started. *Did anyone hear what Houston said at the end? To me?*

Nope! said Yata enthusiastically. *You really took one for the team there, Yuki.*

Yeah, she said distantly. *I hope so.*

What was it about? he asked, slightly more hesitant.

I... hope we don't have to find out.

Uhhh... he seemed to consider pursuing the topic before deciding to move on. *Cool. So who gets to decide which one of these guys fills the power vacuum?*

They won't, she said, looking around at the surrendered soldiers and officials that lined the gangways. *Not here... It's time to return this nation to its people.*

As the day turned to evening, Alkonoth and Ganejin traveled north to bury the warheads underneath the mountains where they could never be uncovered by humans again.

Under the watch of Narajin and Jhalaragon, the citizens and soldiers of the upper echelons of the LCC filed out of the gate and into the desert. When the sun had descended into the west and the structure had been emptied and the refugees headed east toward the other Laurentian towns, the two kaiju turned toward the lights on the northern horizon.

The former citizens of the lower level had made camp in the foothills of the mountains. Upon their arrival at the edge of the makeshift settlement, the kaiju were greeted with silence. Yuki and Yata disembarked and approached the crowd in their human forms. The elderly man who came to greet them seemed to be a community leader, as he chose to speak for them all.

"We're mighty grateful for your help," he said to them. "Houston was no favorite among us... but our homes are gone now, and we can't go back."

"But..." said Yuki, "you have the entire city. You can live in the upper levels."

The man shook his head and looked down at his feet, sighing.

"We just want to live in peace. We'll find a home to the north, on the other side of the mountains. I hear there's green country up that ways, and we may find a place to make our lives."

He looked off at the smoking LCC.

"We ain't going back to that ruin," he continued. "Even if we did find a way to make it livable again, the army would just come back and take it from us, and probably find some way to blame us for what happened. That place is just a reminder of the old world that blew itself up. Those who live in it are cursed to follow their footsteps."

Yuki hesitated a moment, unsure of what to make of his reaction, then nodded.

"Look, we are happy to be rid of Houston," he said. "we thank you for that – and for stopping the war. But now we need to go our own way."

"Then may you find the life you seek," said Yuki. "Mokwa will be with you whenever you need her."

She handed the man the amulet she had found at the lake. He looked at it for a moment, then smiled.

"We'll find someone who can make use of this," he said. "You can be sure that it'll be used wisely."

With that, the man turned his back to the Pantheon and headed back into the camp.

"Uh..." Yata whispered, "are you sure you should be giving him that?"

"I trust them," she said, "they're not power hungry like Houston."

"If you say so... The Laurentian military still has strongholds throughout the country, and it's only a small matter of time until they sweep in and retake control."

"Then they've got the right idea leaving this place. The land to the south is still the Laurentian Empire, just without the world-ending strength that Houston had."

"How do we know that? They don't have Mokwa anymore, and she'll do what she can to keep them from attacking anyone, but... How do you know they won't build another bomb? A closed-off military state that has every reason to hate us isn't exactly a perfect outcome."

"Then whatever happens, we'll have to make sure they can't come back here."

The two of them henshined back into their respective kaiju and turned back toward the LCC as they were joined by Alkonoth, Mokwa, and Ganejin as they returned from the mountains.

Well, said Yata, *just to make sure none of Houston's apocalypse mongering survives.*

Just to be safe, said Ivan.

In perfect synchronization, the Pantheon fired their energy weapons at the center tower, destroying the structure and causing it to collapse onto itself. On its way down it knocked against the surrounding towers, soon causing them all to collapse into a massive cloud of flame and debris. As the smoke cleared, the LCC was gone. The once mighty empire had been toppled and the machine of war had finally ground to a halt.

Well, that's it, said Yuki. *Let's go home.*

Which home are we talking about? asked Manny.

Surprised at his question, she realized she wasn't sure how to respond. They had gone through so much together that it felt strange even thinking about returning to Narai.

I guess... she said, *our real homes.*

Do they even want the kaiju back? asked Yata.

We might have to lay low... Not tell anyone that we're, you know, kaiju. But we should see the people we miss... The people we did all of this for.

Well... said Ivan, *I guess we say goodbye.*

Yeah, said Yata. *Oh, screw this, let's get out. I wanna hug you guys.*

Four lights flashed and the members of the Pantheon appeared on the surface of the desert. Yata ran up to Manny first and pulled him close to his chest.

"I'm gonna miss you, my dude," the Tarakonan warrior said.

"I'm gonna miss you too... My dude!"

Next was Yuki. He almost said something, but they ended up just sharing a silent nod. All the better, she thought, as she could feel the lump in her throat and the tears beginning to well up.

Finally he came to Ivan. As he went in for the hug, the Scythian former enemy swept him up in his arms and planted an intensely amorous, open-mouthed kiss square on his lips. Yata's entire body went limp, his face collapsing into a pile of mush as it was smushed against his surly friend's. After a long moment, Ivan quickly drew his face away, Yata standing there with a look of perplexed shock and a quivering smile beginning to form.

"I'm sorry," Ivan said in his usual matter-of-fact tone.

"N-no…" Yata stammered, "I just didn't know you –"

"Have a husband," Ivan finished the sentence, his cheeks blushing while he tried to maintain his serious demeanor.

"Oh…" Yata's face went from excited surprise, to disappointment, to general amusement in the span of about three seconds.

"I have been away for too long…" said Ivan. "But I will see my family again soon."

"Well, I'm sure they'll be just as happy to see you," said Yata, smiling and placing a hand on his shoulder.

"I will miss all of you," Ivan said to his companions, turning to each of them. "I am glad you accepted me after what I did before. I am glad that we're friends."

"Any time, buddy," said Yuki, a smile spread across her face.

With one last tearful look at each other, the Pantheon Colossi henshined back into their kaiju and set out to the west. They had been irrevocably bonded by their adventure, and Yuki knew it would certainly not be the last time they would see each other. Until then, it was time to go home.

Chapter 20:
Daikaiju Yuki

After the long trek to the western barrier of the Laurentian continent, stopping along the way to pay their respects at the burial mound and saying farewell to Mokwa as she returned to the northern wilderness, the Pantheon Colossi went their separate ways.

Yata and Jhalaragon swam back toward Tarakona, Yata spouting something about wanting to go on another adventure after stopping at home.

What are you gonna do? he had asked Yuki.

Me? Go to sleep, probably, she joked. *Then... I dunno... but I'm feeling pretty good. Maybe I'll conquer the world.*

Yikes, laughed Yata, nervously.

I mean, let's not get ahead of ourselves, she laughed back.

Ivan and Alkonoth flew back to Scythia, although he wasn't sure how they'd deal with his status as a deserter – probably not too harshly, he mused, as the government had other things to worry about after spending years in a futile war that had gained them nothing and lost them the support of most of the populace. Above all, he looked forward to seeing his husband and adopted son again.

Manny and Ganejin took a sub-ocean volcanic fissure into the mantle and back to the island off the coast of Avarta. He was sure his parents had missed him, and he knew that after everything he had been through, he could help them to have a better life, even if they would never believe his story.

As for Yuki and Narajin, they swam day and night straight across the Pacific until the shores of the distant island chain became visible. For the first time since setting out on their quest, they were seeing their home, the beautiful country of Narai.

Making sure to come ashore in a rural area close to the inland sea so as not to draw any unwanted attention, they sat down in the middle of a field, the first snow of the season beginning to drift and shimmer through the air and coat the bare trees. In a flash of light and energy, Yuki found herself standing on the ground next to the red lion kaiju, her slippers crunching on the snow-covered grass.

It was only then that she realized that after all they had been through, she had never been in human form long enough to have time to change her clothes.

I did all of that in my pajamas, she laughed to Narajin, clutching her amulet. *What's wrong with me?*

Nothing, he said, his booming, ancient-sounding tone seemingly hiding a layer of emotion. *It is actually quite impressive.*

She looked up at him, white snow landing on his dark red fur. He looked majestic, she thought, truly worthy of being called a god as much he was worthy of being called her friend.

Snow... he said, looking off into the flurries. *That is what your name means.*

Really? I mean, I think I knew that.

An ancient language, still a part of this culture, and a part of you. A fine tradition to uphold.

Tears seemed to be welling up in his giant feline eyes.

When do you think we'll see each other next? she asked.

Oh, I will be around. Whenever you would like, really. I only hope that our next adventure is instigated by less dire circumstances.

You and me both, she said. *I'm sure we'll get everyone back together when the time's right for it.*

That we will, he said.

He looked down at her and squinted his eyes, an expression she assumed was his closest approximation of smiling. She smiled back at him and realized that she was crying, too.

Wow, this is weird. I never cry, she said, wiping the tears off of her cheeks.

Yuki, he said, his voice completely open and earnest, *I want you to know that I could not have done any of that without you – and through it all, I am glad to be your cat.*

That was what pushed her over the edge. Tears streamed down her face as she ran forward and hugged his knee with the entire span of her arms, still clutching the amulet in her hand.

I'm glad you're my cat, too, she sobbed. *You're the best cat ever.*

Let us not get carried away, now, he said half-jokingly.

She stepped back and wiped her eyes, which were still welling up.

I guess I'll see you later, then? she sniffled.

You certainly will, Yuki. Good luck on your journey.

With that, he stood up and turned, heavy footfalls carrying him slowly into the now-thick snowfall. His silhouette faded until finally it was gone, blocked by a sheet of falling white crystals. She stood there for a moment, considering just fusing back into him, but quickly decided against it. It was time to start making her way back to the capital, and hopefully find a change of clothes. Turning around, she walked off into the snow in the other direction.

To her luck, she soon came across a road and was able to hitch a ride on a cart carrying beer to the capital. The driver was kind enough to share some of it with her, which made the passage of time much more bearable. In just less than four hours, they reached the outer limits of Narai City.

It looked even more beautiful than she had remembered, aside from the area still being rebuilt from her debacle of a first experience in the body of a kaiju. Memories of the incident brought her momentary embarrassment and guilt, but it appeared that everyone was getting on with their lives and greeted her cheerfully. The driver soon reminded her that they were in fact happy to see the beer cart and weren't actually waving at her, which lessened her enthusiasm a bit.

When the cart passed the entrance to the temple, she asked the driver to let her off and thanked him for the ride and the beer, both of which had helped considerably. Getting out, she made her way to the main gate, which had been completely restored since her accidental rampage.

The figure of Narajin's statue once more stared down at her from its perch at the center of the arch, bringing a smile to her face as she looked up at it. Funny, she thought, how something can have an entirely different meaning once it becomes more familiar.

Making her way up the path to the temple, the cherry blossoms had been replaced by sheets of frozen white lining the branches and sprinkling the ground. Looking ahead, she saw a figure standing outside in the snow, walking amongst the area where the garden had been in warmer weather. As she drew nearer, she realized that it was the Priestess. She looked as beautiful as ever in her white kimono, matching the snow perfectly and accenting it with its pattern of pink flowers. Despite the fact that she had thought of her as a friend and a warm reminder of home, the amount that Yuki had thought about her on her journey was indicative that the woman she had known only a brief time occupied a place in her mind reserved for something a bit more.

The Priestess turned and noticed Yuki, still about twenty meters away. A smile began to form on the woman's face, letting her know that her reservations were unwarranted.

"Yuki!" she shouted, waving.

"Uh... Hi!" Yuki yelled back, continuing towards her.

When they were in a reasonable range of each other just in front of the temple steps, they stopped. Yuki half expected to go in for a hug, but stopped herself.

"Yuki, it's good to see you again," the Priestess said, smiling.

"It's... good to see you too!"

They stood in silence for a second before Yuki continued.

"Sorry, I've been... away."

The Priestess laughed gently and put her hand on Yuki's shoulder before taking it away.

"I know..."

Confused, Yuki tried to think of a way to respond, but the ability to construct words had left her.

"Don't worry," the Priestess continued, "no one else knows. I'm not even sure if anyone else noticed you were gone, with all the commotion about Narajin's return and disappearance."

"Uh... What?"

"Oh, wow, that sounds terrible," she said, visibly blushing. "What I mean is, everyone at the temple... Here, walk with me."

Putting her hand gently on Yuki's back, they walked through the winter garden.

"A lot has changed since you've been gone. When the war ended, the Emperor disbanded the military leaders after their corruption started to come to light – which is to say, I think you've been unofficially pardoned."

"Oh... Well, that's good."

"I wouldn't recommend seeing him about it, of course. The reception to Narajin's awakening has been..."

"I figured. Besides... I've had enough of emperors."

"What about me?" the woman teased. "I might not have a ton of power, but I am in charge here."

"That's different."

Yuki still wasn't entirely sure how to respond to the woman next to her, someone who clearly knew more about her than she was letting on, but was unequivocally on her side – a rare thing indeed.

"In case you were wondering," the Priestess continued, "the reason I didn't tell you about the henshin ceremony was that the military was planning to force our hand in..."

"...taking control of Narajin," Yuki finished. "I found out from... well, I found out. That's what Ken Sakurai was here to do."

She inhaled sharply before continuing. It was time to get straight what had transpired once and for all.

"About Ken..."

"I killed him," the Priestess cut to the point.

Yuki's eyes flew wide open as the two women stopped and turned to look at each other.

"You... what?"

"I killed him. I did what I had to do. And you, I imagine, would've done the same."

On some level, Yuki expected to feel horror at the revelation. Instead, she felt a kind of knowing respect. This was a woman who would do what was necessary to stop far worse things from happening – a trait they shared. If anything, it made her like her more.

"I'm sure he had it coming," replied Yuki, a grin forming through the shock.

Smiling, the Priestess looked down at the path before they resumed their walk.

"There were rumors of Narajin and Ganejin appearing in Avarta," she continued. "Then there was the volcano in Tarakona, and some said kaiju had something to do with it... But that is how legends go. Even softer were the whispers of something big happening on the far side of the world."

Swallowing hard, Yuki tried to anticipate where the conversation was going to no avail.

"What I mean to say," said the Priestess, "is that here in Narai, life goes on. People don't know that the kaiju saved the world in any real way, only that the war ended and they can now live in a land of peace. But isn't that what it's about?"

They stopped, the Priestess turning to Yuki.

"I've never been a fighter," she said, "but I'd imagine that this is what people fight for, when it's for the right reasons."

"That's... actually pretty accurate," said Yuki, her heartbeat beginning to even out.

"I'm glad," the Priestess said, smiling, "please stop me if I ever spout off about something I know nothing about."

"I'll do that," she responded before she even thought about what she was saying.

The mysterious woman looked down and chuckled again, before turning her gaze back to Yuki.

"There was one person who came looking for you. I think you know, and I think you should go to see her."

Yuki instantly knew who she was talking about. A strange feeling, both warm and nervous, began to flow through her.

"I'd better," she said. "I hope I see you again."

"Oh, I'd imagine you will," the Priestess said, flashing another knowing smile before turning and walking back toward the temple.

As Yuki turned toward the road, she felt like there was more that she wanted to say. Taking a deep breath, she spun back around.

"Priestess," she said, causing the woman to stop and turn back toward her gracefully, an attentive expression awaiting Yuki's final question. "What... I mean, if you don't mind me asking, what's your name? I'm guessing it's not Priestess."

A charming smile grew cross the woman's face, an alluring look in her eyes.

"Midori," she said.

For a moment they stood perfectly still, sharing each other's gaze. Then, still smiling, Midori turned back toward the pagoda. Yuki considered calling after her, but decided that more progress could be made another day as their reunion had already gone far better than she had expected. Her heart fluttering, she watched as the woman glided away through the particles of falling white. At last, beaming, she put her back to the temple.

"Midori..." she whispered to herself.

Trudging through the snow back toward the road, Yuki knew exactly where she had to go. She followed it for several kilometers, the light beginning to dim until streetlamps were the only source of illumination. Soon, she found herself on a quiet, familiar street – one she hadn't visited for a long time. At the beginning of the next block was a house, lit from within, the sight of which brought a flood of memories and nostalgia surging through her.

She walked up to it and prepared to knock on the door, beginning to brush the snow off of her clothes before realizing that she would look somewhat ridiculous no matter what. She knocked, and the sound of pattering footsteps approached. Slowly, it cracked open, revealing a face that Yuki had deeply missed.

"Hi Mom," she said.

"Yuki?" her mother gasped. "Is that really you?"

"Yeah, it's me!" she said, throwing her arms out to the sides.

Her mother threw herself forward and embraced her, holding on for what seemed like an entire minute as they stood in the doorway.

"Mom, I think we should go inside," Yuki laughed.

"Yes. Yes! Come in!"

Yuki took her slippers off as she entered, looking around to see a warm, inviting home, the place she had lived with her mother and father as a child.

"Why are you wearing pajamas?" her mother asked, sounding and looking confused.

"It's... a really long story."

"Well, that's fine, but let's find you something else. You look like you're about to freeze."

"Mom, really, I'm fine. I mean, yeah. I should probably change."

While her mother prepared an impromptu dinner for two, Yuki slipped into her bedroom to find that most of her old things were almost exactly where she had left them, if moved slightly for cleaning. Her eyes drifted to the book lying on her bedside table – The Story of the Pantheon Colossi.

Unbelievable, she thought.

Opening her closet, she found several light, nice-looking kimonos that she probably hadn't worn since she was a teenager. Fortunately they still fit, and as soon as she had slipped into a bright pink yukata, she was able to step out into their main room where her mother was placing two bowls of udon on either side of their table.

"Aww, thank you!" she said, acknowledging that her mother had made her favorite noodles.

"Sit down!" her mother said as they sat themselves on either side.

Yuki began slurping up the noodles voraciously.

"Wow," she said, her mouth still full, "I don't think I've eaten anything this good in months."

It didn't take her long to realize that she hadn't been eating at all recently, just absorbing mana through the kaiju. Being in human form did have its perks.

"So..." her mother began cautiously, "what have you been up to recently?"

"Um..." Yuki started, slurping a noodle and thinking while she chewed.

"It took me so long to find out that you had been discharged, so I went to the temple, but you weren't there."

"Yeah... Uh, I went away for a while."

"Away? What were you doing?"

"You know, saving civilization. Stopping a war. Fighting monsters. The usual."

Clearly baffled, her mother still managed to put on a smile.

"I know you would make your father proud – and you make me proud."

Swallowing her food and putting down her chopsticks, Yuki looked at her mother. It seemed like it should've been a sarcastic response to someone who had come back from who-knows-where doing who-knows-what, but as far as she knew, her mother was incapable of sarcasm and her smile looked completely sincere.

"Do you really mean that?"

"Of course I do. I think he would absolutely support you in... Whatever it is you're doing. Which is... What, again?"

Beaming, Yuki tried to find a way to say what she was about to say delicately, before realizing that there was absolutely no delicate way to say it.

"I'm a... daikaiju."

Slowly, her mother's eyebrows raised in surprise, hanging there for a few seconds before she burst out laughing, covering her mouth in embarrassment.

"I know," said Yuki, "it sounds ridiculous –"

"No," her mother said, stifling her laughter, "it's just not what I expected. That's... Well, I don't know what to say. It's quite... Something, certainly."

Yuki chuckled, smiled, and went back to slurping her udon. A strange, unfamiliar feeling began to wash over her. It wasn't bad, just different. It felt like, for the first time in her life, she knew exactly who she was, and everything was going to be okay. As she sat in her mother's house eating noodles, she knew that she had brought the human race back from the edge of doom.

Through all the times she had been made to feel worthless, to feel like she was a failure, she wished she could have had a glimpse of what she was feeling in that moment. Placing her hand on the amulet in her pocket, she reached out to the giant lion who many looked upon as a god.

Thanks for everything, she thought to him.

Of course, Yuki.

No matter how few knew it, a small woman from Narai was in fact an unstoppable force of nature, a towering behemoth of immeasurable power who fought to defend life on Earth. She had flown over oceans and swum through volcanos. She had fought terrible beasts from the depths of hell and defended millions from forces beyond their understanding. Moreover, she liked it.

Daikaiju Yuki, she thought. *Cool.*

The ? End

Yuki returns in
Y2K: YUKI CONQUERS THE WORLD